Her Music Masters
Pleasure Island Book Two

By

Anya Summers

Published by Blushing Books®,
a subsidiary of

ABCD Graphics and Design
977 Seminole Trail #233
Charlottesville, VA 22901

The trademark Blushing Books® is registered in the US Patent and Trademark Office.

Anya Summers
Her Music Masters

Print ISBN: 978-1-61258-174-3
Cover Art by ABCD Graphics & Design

Chapter One

September

"You are no daughter of mine."

Those words were emblazoned upon Amaya's soul. Two weeks. It had taken a mere two weeks for her entire world to collapse. When Amaya contemplated the full scope of the ramifications, she sank into a depression so dark as to be an antithesis to light.

She was drowning in a quagmire of her own making. Amaya had been foolish, she'd been careless with who knew about her lifestyle, and because of that utter lack of restraint, her world no longer existed.

Every time she glanced at her violin case, she felt sick to her stomach. Every time she thought about the images that had been emailed to every member of the London Symphony Orchestra, despair threatened to choke her. Every time she remembered the bleak disappointment on her mother's face, and her father's dispassionate grimace, she caved in on herself.

The boat swayed as it moved with the ocean swells. Amaya stared out across the endless deep blue waves, searching for peace, searching for a passion to continue putting one foot in front of the other, searching for a way to survive the destruction and ruin her life had become. Her large sunglasses shielded her eyes from the bright midday glare and gave her the appearance, she hoped, of an aloof tourist. They were a ruse, for when she glimpsed herself in a mirror, her eyes looked haunted even to her.

The ivory ship, a large catamaran style vessel, with sleek lines that shimmered in the sun and was dubbed *Goddess of the Sea*, moved through the water like a hungry sea creature after its prey. At the helm was Deke. He was every inch a Dom and this was obvious in all he did, from the way he carried himself, to the way he steered his ship, as if he would make the ocean bend to his will alone. Amaya could spot a Dom from a hundred yards away. As a lifelong submissive, she respected and acknowledged Deke's dominance. But that was all. She would not submit to him.

It wasn't that she didn't find him attractive. With his tall, lanky body that was more muscle than bone, and dark hair tinged with sunlight and windblown, he was an attractive man who should make her want to beg for his touch.

But she wasn't interested. In anyone. Or anything, if she was honest.

The island speared up out of the ocean like a defiant warrior against the tide. Pristine white sand glimmered in the noonday sun. A single mountain peak ascended toward the heavens, adorned in green foliage. The ivory dome of the hotel was like a beacon for weary travelers.

Deke steered them into the tiny inlet bay to the docks. Unlike at Nassau, the docks here were nearly vacant. Oh, there were people here, for sure. Amaya had spied a few couples on the beach and noticed workers milling about, but the hustle and bustle of Nassau was thankfully absent. Amaya didn't want to deal with people. She didn't want to face the betrayal. She didn't want to feel anything. All she wanted was to escape the shattered remnants of her life and to be left in peace.

Once the ship was safely docked, Amaya gathered her things and couldn't prevent her sneer as she glanced at her violin case. The damn thing had brought her nothing but agony. If it weren't for the rather hefty sum she'd paid for it, she would be rid of it. Maybe she should contact one of the instrument dealers she knew well and have them sell it. It wasn't like she had a job to go to where she needed to play. And in her world, word spread like a flaming match tossed onto nitroglycerin. Everyone who was anyone in her circle knew about her fall from grace. Which meant that no one in her field would hire her.

Amaya had not played a single note since her life had imploded. And she didn't know if she would ever play again. Music that had always been a comfort and a catharsis for her was now tainted and stained. Instead of joy, there was a well of sorrow that was deeper than any ocean.

A young bellhop took her luggage and pointed her in the direction of a slight, dark-haired woman standing at the path to the hotel. She was perhaps as short as Amaya was herself, topping out at only five feet. She had black hair that fell to the middle of her back but that was where any similarity ended. Amaya wasn't necessarily flat chested. She did fill a B cup, but in no way was she as well endowed. Whereas the other woman was trim, but voluptuous where it counted. She wore a form-fitting blouse and pencil skirt showcasing her body. Amaya was instantly jealous. She'd always wished her body had more va-va-voom to it. She had curves, but they were slight, and depending on what she wore, they could look nonexistent. If she put her hair up in a ball cap she could be mistaken for a man—and had been, a time or two.

"Welcome to Pleasure Island. I'm Yvette, and if you will all follow me in to the registration desk, we will get you folks situated in your rooms," the woman said.

Amaya waited, allowing the couples to file in first, and then she followed in the rear of the group. This was so she wouldn't have to converse with anyone. Their excitement over the island was palpable. It just made her stomach roil. There was a beach. There was water. There was a blue sky. But none of it touched her.

It was like the music in her soul, in her heart, had died two weeks ago and she didn't know if she would get it back.

Yvette was in the process of describing the different features of the island; the pool, beach chaises, marina with ski boat rentals, the newly added deep sea fishing tours, the restaurant, the new pizza parlor, the club. On and on she prattled, and Amaya was so tired. She just wanted her key and a bed. Inside, her sandals clicked against the marble flooring. She glanced around at the understated opulence. They had spared no expense on this place. And if she didn't feel dead inside, she'd be oohing and aahing with the rest of the new guests.

"Amaya. It's a pleasure to see you, lass," a deep, cultured baritone with a hint of a Scottish accent said while she was waiting in line at the registration desk.

Amaya turned, plastering a smile on her face, and spied the owner and operator of Pleasure Island, Jared McTavish. He had an easy smile and was what her friend Delilah would call 'downright fuckable.' The two of them had never dallied with each other—not that she would have turned the towering hunk down—they had both been with other people when they did cross paths. She bowed her head in respect. "Master Jared. It's good to see you."

He enveloped her in a warm hug. And she just stood there, awkwardly, sort of hugging him back. She tried to loosen up a bit so that she wasn't so stiff. But she was holding herself together by a thread here. If she felt comfort of any kind, she couldn't be responsible for her actions. Like bawling all over his dark pinstripe dress shirt.

He released her from his friendly embrace and nodded toward the second registration agent helping Yvette get all the newcomers situated. Her bouncy red curls swayed every time she moved her head. "I see Miriam is getting you settled."

"Yes, she is. This place is wonderful, Master J. I'm looking forward to staying here." *And likely burrowing in my hotel room like a deranged sociopath*, but on the scale of worrisome activities, it could be worse—like, say, a game of Russian Roulette.

"Thank you kindly. I do hope you will enjoy your stay with us. Be sure to read through the sub packet that is included with your reservation," Jared said.

"I will. Delilah told me that you are no longer living the bachelor life." Not that it would matter. Amaya wasn't here for a relationship or hot sweaty bouts of sex, although that might be one way to work through her malaise.

A smile spread over his face. "And you heard right. Why don't you have dinner with my sub Naomi and me sometime this week? We can catch up. I will have my secretary contact you to set it up. I'm late for a meeting now or I would stay."

6

"I understand you're working. It was good seeing you. I look forward to it." Amaya nodded, her stomach tied in knots.

"Maybe we will see you in the club tonight, too."

"Maybe," she said, as noncommittally as possible. She wasn't going anywhere near the club. She wasn't here to sate her submissive appetite. She was here to hide away from the rest of the world until the dust from the nuclear explosion of her life settled.

"Good. Enjoy the island. I will see you later, lass."

"Okay. Bye." Her shoulders relaxed a bit as he strode away. She didn't want to be analyzed by a Dom or comforted by one. One of the reasons Jared was such a good Dom was because he took the time to investigate and uncover a sub's hurts. Amaya didn't want that, and had just had one hell of a time pretending her heart wasn't in a million pieces. What she wanted was to be left alone. Once she was safely ensconced within her hotel room, she didn't have to come out for any reason and could order all her meals to her room. Easy, simple, no stress.

She had paid in full for the next three weeks. She had three weeks to decide what to do with the rest of her life. Without music, she had no clue. It wasn't like there a handbook, 'What to Do When You Ruin Your Life for Dummies,' that would help her steer a new course. The problem was that if she were a ship, her rudder was broken, her navigation equipment had quit working, and the hull was sinking.

"And here is the submissive packet of materials that Master J mentioned. Please be sure to read it fully before entering the club or any of the facilities. Your cuffs, should you choose to wear them, are in your room. Now yours as a guest are red, with the white island logo on them. We color code here to make it easier. If I could have you sign on the line here? And then here is your keypad code for you to use to access your room, charge meals in the restaurant, enter the pool area, marina rentals, and such," Miriam said.

"Thank you."

"It's my pleasure. Sean has already delivered your luggage to your room. Do you have any questions?" Miriam's curls bounced. Amaya felt like she was on a tilt-a-whirl, where the bright flashing lights and multitude of sounds were pressing in on her. It was all too much and she needed to get to the safety of her room, pronto.

"No, thank you." She took everything from Miriam's hands, clutching the key to her room like a lifeline. She just had to go a little bit farther and then she could burrow.

"Enjoy your stay with us." Miriam's bright red curls bounced even more as she nodded her head.

Amaya escaped the front desk chaos, gripping the papers. Feeling the edges of a panic attack, she used every reserve of strength she possessed to keep going. Once she was in her room, then she could fall apart. She rode the elevator to the sixth floor and exited into the airy hall with sky blue walls and white paneling. Her feet clicked over the ivory marble floors. At any other time in her life, she would be charmed by the luxurious décor, but as it was, it was too bright, too cheerful, and it was making her dizzy.

Her room number, six-zero-nine, was one of the corner suites that overlooked the bay.

She entered the room, barely registering the beautiful fixtures, from the wooden floor to the canopy bed and the small kitchen. She slid the bolt home in the door after she spied her luggage in the corner as promised. She dropped the stack of paperwork on the coffee table and headed toward the bed.

Amaya stripped as she walked, letting her clothing lie where it fell, and then climbed into bed. She wasn't hungry, or curious about the island. All she was, was past the point of exhaustion. She pulled the covers up over her head.

And, for the next seventy-two hours, that was where Amaya stayed.

*****

On the morning of her fourth day on the island, Amaya knew instinctively she had to leave her room. As much as it pained her to do it, if she stayed, Jared would be knocking down her door and trying to dissect her feelings. She didn't want that. All she wanted to do was to lick her wounds in peace.

So, after a brief breakfast, she left her room, avoiding the club, pool, marina, and restaurant—anywhere there might actually be people—and hiked around the island until she came upon a small, enclosed section of beach that was far away from everyone. It was separated from the rest of the beach on the southernmost point of the island by giant rock formations that were part of an ancient lava bed before the island volcano went dormant. It was off the inlaid path by about a mile, which meant the likelihood of anyone traveling in this direction was minimal at best.

It gave her a little peace of mind, knowing she wouldn't be disturbed. Every day, she would sit in the sand, her toes touching the tide as it swelled and ebbed along the shore, and watch the ocean as it moved.

She still couldn't seem to cry over everything. Amaya wondered whether she should be concerned that she couldn't seem to feel anything but then the thought would leave as she watched a seagull cry as it dove into the surf and emerged with a fish clamped within its beak.

Amaya developed a pattern. Every morning after she had breakfast delivered, she headed to what she had begun to consider her spot on the island, and there she would stay until the sun began to set. She would then hike back to the hotel, have dinner in her room, and go to bed. She avoided the club. She avoided people in general. But she was surviving, she was alive, and if she couldn't seem to feel anything about any subject, well, that was easier than delving into the vast wasteland of her emotions.

Life wasn't perfect. She received funny looks from the Doms she passed, concern dotting their gazes, but she quickly and soundly dismissed it—and them. She wasn't interested in connecting and having the heart to heart talks that Doms were so fond of as they tried to fix what was wrong. This was something not one of them could fix. She had to do it, only she had no idea how, or even the inclination to try.

Amaya didn't want to need anyone. On the tenth day of her stay, she exited the elevator and ran smack dab into a muscular male body.

"Whoa, steady there," said the familiar baritone; one that had visited her in her dreams.

Amaya lifted her glance, up and up, and found herself staring into cerulean blue eyes that reminded her of the ocean on her beach. Lachlin O'Toole stood there, his blond hair a bit longer than the last time they had crossed paths, and at his side, his partner Jax Holiday, his black hair artfully arranged in a rakish fashion. These two Doms could

11

melt the panties off any sub, as they had done with hers almost a year ago at the McDougal wedding. Lachlin, with his towering six-foot frame, gave her a warm smile bursting with remembrance.

"Amaya, we didn't realize you would be here, lovely," Jax murmured, and she shifted her gaze, taking in his scruffy, dark, five o'clock shadow, a devil-may-care smile shrouding his succulent lips. He was a few inches shorter than his partner, but next to her they were both behemoths.

She plastered a fake smile on her face, wanting to curse the heavens that of all the places for her to run into them, it had to be here, and it had to be now. She answered, fluttering her lashes and casting her gaze down in respect, "I'm taking some time away from work. How are you?"

That was her story and she was sticking to it. The less people knew about her imploded life, the less likely it was that she would have to field questions.

"Same. Bastian and Delilah are moving in together now that our tour has finished. If you haven't heard, Bastian proposed and Delilah said yes," Jax said.

Amayah had heard. And she was so happy for Delilah after all the crud she'd been through. She and Bastian were perfect for one another. It did Amaya's heart good to know that happiness could be found, even through the darkest times. It was what kept her going; that hope that it would work out, like it had with Delilah.

She said, "Delilah told me that. I think it's wonderful that they are engaged."

"Not to change the subject, but will you be at the club this evening?" Lachlin asked, stroking his hand down her arm.

Deflect, deflect, deflect. "Maybe. I'm not sure," she said, not committing but not letting them think she was blowing them off. She was blowing everyone off, she just didn't want them to feel bad about it.

Lachlin said, "You should come. It would be great to get re-acquainted with you."

"Um, sure. That would be nice. I need to go." Amaya excused herself and walked away, feeling their gazes boring holes in her back as she escaped their sexy invitation. What were they doing here? Why did they have to be here?

Had she pissed off some demi-god who was now making it his mission to see that everything from her past was dragged up from perdition to torture her with? The three of them had experienced a scorching night of passion at Declan and Zoey McDougal's wedding the previous year. Since then, that night had been in the back of her mind and the two Doms had played starring roles in her dreams on more than one occasion.

It was one the reasons why she had visited the club in Amsterdam a month ago in the first place. She was normally so careful with her desires and keeping her lifestyle separate from her work that she rarely headed to a BDSM club while on tour with the orchestra. But she had woken up achy and needy because she had dreamed about that glorious night and had needed relief that no vibrator in the world could provide. Once you have had two men take you beyond the edge of passion, nothing else ever quite satisfies you the way that did.

It was during that outing that Amaya had been followed—unbeknownst to her—and it had tanked her career and her life. How could she get over the past and move on if her wildest fantasies appeared on the island looking like two rock 'n' roll sex gods, and made the emotions she would rather keep under lock and key rattle their damn chains?

Amaya worried that she wouldn't be able to resist the temptation if presented with another opportunity to sleep with them. It had been far and away the best sex of her life. There was no comparison. Even with her battered and bruised heart, her body was still susceptible to the erotic thrall they presented. Her panties were wet and her nipples ached to feel their mouths. What did that say about her as a person, not just a submissive, that she was so easily tempted by them?

And why oh why had her island escape become her prison?

Chapter Two

Lachlin O'Toole watched the slight swish of Amaya Tenaka's jean-clad hips as she exited the hotel. The wounded expression in her midnight eyes cut through the heart of him. Where was the vivacious, seductive enchantress they had met in Scotland last year? He had never forgotten that one night with her, try as he might. As much as he loved his partner, Jax Holiday, having Amaya join them had been one of the hottest, most mind-bending experiences of his life and it had ignited a dream he continued to hold that he hadn't even hoped was possible.

Ever since their little escapade, he had endeavored to convince Jax that they needed a submissive to complement and enhance their relationship. Jax wanted nothing to do with adding a woman to the mix. He enjoyed topping a woman with Lachlin at a club but he didn't want one thrown into their daily lives. Lachlin, on the other hand, yearned for a woman to make their duo a triad. He and Jax had been partners for going on thirteen years. At thirty-five, Lachlin was feeling the need for continuance and he just wanted more. It didn't mean he loved Jax any less.

And there had been something about Amaya's sweet surrender that night which had touched the very heart of him. Jax tossed an arm about his shoulders.

"Maybe we can have another go with the pretty violinist tonight, yeah?" Jax said as they made their way to one of the golf carts and headed to their private villa.

It was a beautiful place, Pleasure Island. Jared had invested not just in the big picture of the place, but every minute detail. The main hotel was gorgeous. But the Master stations along the paths to the villas and around the island were inspired. Lachlin could tell by the wicked gleam in Jax's eyes that he was making plans to utilize every facility on the island until their cocks shriveled up and fell off from over use. Lachlin was all for it, as long as those plans included the delectable Amaya.

Their villa was secluded and off the beaten path. The ivory dome rose out of a profusion of palm trees and flowing bushes. Lachlin really wasn't much of a gardener and couldn't name a single flower, but the effect it created in its totality was stunning. Lachlin wanted to check his keyboard and ensure that nothing had happened to it during their travels. It wasn't that he didn't trust Jared's staff, but he needed his keyboard for when the mood to play struck. Jax was the same way about his bass guitar, so Lachlin knew he wasn't a complete head case.

Inside their villa, the hardwood floors stretched throughout the place. The eat-in kitchen was modern, with white cabinets and dark gray marble countertops. Lachlin went directly to his keyboard case which had been propped against a wall in the living room, winding his way around the chocolate leather couch and loveseat. He noted the innocuous hideaway loops on the ends of the coffee table. Jared was a bloody brilliant Master, he had to give him that. Lachlin would never have thought about adding that extra touch. He wondered who Jared's furniture dealer was. He and Jax had been needing some upgrades in the furniture department.

Once he was sure his baby was in perfect working order, Lachlin set it up in the living room. He needed it in case he awoke in the middle of the night with a melody he had to get down. It had happened on too many occasions to count. He turned and spotted Jax in the dungeon. He liked the open air format of the place. The California king size four-poster bed with its fluffy white bedding was sure to get a workout while they were here. In the miniature dungeon area, which was roughly the size of a walk-in closet, stood a single bondage horse. Granted, it looked like there was a station against the wall with hooks for a Dom to attach a sub's cuffs to. Jax stood there, stroking the padded leather. This villa had been dubbed 'Blow Job Heaven' due to the bondage horse in the private dungeon. If there was one thing Jax loved receiving, it was a good blow job. Lachlin's mouth watered at the thought. He loved giving them, so it worked out well.

"Take a piss if you need to, then I want your ass up on that horse," Jax ordered him, and Lachlin felt knots form in his gut. As much as Lachlin loved and needed to dominate, Jax made him willing to submit to anything he had in mind. Jax's demeanor sharpened into his 'don't mess with me' Dom mode. Lachlin groaned deep in his chest when he noticed the bulge in Jax's pants. Jax had quite the package. He wasn't long, but his cock was almost as thick as a baseball bat.

"And if I don't?" Lachlin teased. It was a long-standing game between them that ensured Jax drew out the torture a wee bit, and in the end fucked Lachlin until his legs gave out. It was incredible.

"Then I won't let you come and you will have to attend the club, blue balls and all," Jax seethed. Jax was the hot head in the relationship, with Lachlin being the one to bring him back when he went into one of his zero-to-pissed-off modes. Jax lived for the control and order, and when it wasn't obeyed, there was very little he wouldn't try to punish a naughty sub.

With no further urging needed, Lachlin did as he was bid and shucked his clothes during the walk from the living room to the dungeon, not minding where the clothes fell as he prowled. His cock bobbed and strained for Jax's deft touch as he padded toward the horse.

18

Jax had wasted no time in disrobing and joined him. Before Lachlin could mount the horse, Jax yanked him into his arms for a torrid kiss. It was a blistering mingle of tongue and teeth. Lachlin's lips burned as Jax's stubble grazed the sensitive flesh. Jax palmed Lachlin's cock, sliding his deft fingers around the base and squeezing. Lachlin growled into Jax's mouth.

His eyes damn near crossed as Jax stroked him. He couldn't help his involuntary thrust, nor the way he quaked under Jax's touch. Lachlin gripped Jax's bulging member, hungering for the feel of him pumping his thick length in his ass. The only thing that would make it even better would be the sweet fist of Amaya's cunt wrapped around his cock.

Lachlin swore right then and there that he would make it happen.

Jax ripped his mouth from Lachlin's and said, "Get on the bench."

Lachlin didn't need to be told twice. He had barely mounted the black leather, when Jax began restraining his arms and feet. Then Jax caressed the globes of Lachlin's ass, making him squirm and his gut quiver in anticipation. At this rate, he was going to blow his load before Jax even penetrated him. And then Jax was slathering lubricant over Lachlin's puckered hole, inserting two fingers to stretch his ass. Lachlin could tell that Jax was in a hurry after their long travel day to get here. He and

19

Jax weren't public about their relationship—not that they were ashamed of it in the least, but the record company had wanted it kept quiet. The couple did end up coming out, as it were, two, maybe three years previously, but they had spent so long keeping their bedroom activities behind locked doors or in clubs that they still tended to have a no touching policy when they traveled.

Jax needed sex constantly. Not that Lachlin was complaining, and he moaned as Jax pressed a third finger into his ass. His hands fisted in the cuffs at the beautiful pressure building up.

Then Lachlin felt the bulbous head of a plug as Jax inserted it in his ass. It was cone shaped, and widened to the base. Lachlin's tissues stretched to accommodate the girth and then his lover switched the vibrations on. Lachlin grunted at the exquisite torture. Jax put it on a low setting, just enough to set his teeth on edge, but not enough to put him over the top.

And then Lachlin was staring at the glorious sight that was Jax's cock. It was thick, so much so that Lachlin had a hard time even with his piano player hands, wrapping them around Jax's girth when they were free. The crest already had a pearlescent drop of Jax's cream glistening on it and Lachlin licked his lips.

"Oh yeah, and if you suck me real well, I may just give you what you want," Jax said.

Lachlin needed no further urging. He opened his mouth as Jax fit the wide crown inside. He swished his tongue around the underside as Jax thrust, hitting the back of his throat. Lachlin was unable to move as Jax drove his hips and plunged in pistoning thrusts into his mouth. Restrained as he was, all Lachlin could do was accept Jax's shaft. He greedily sucked on his lover's member, just the way he knew would drive Jax crazy. He reveled in the feel of him as Jax shuttled his length in and out.

The buzzing hum of the butt plug sent continual sparks of pleasure straight to Lachlin's cock. It was making him so hard he could likely cut rocks with his dick. Jax gripped his head as he thrust, and Lachlin could imagine the heated look on his face, which only made him work his mouth harder over his cock.

Jax's cock jerked, spewing cum into Lachlin's mouth. He slurped at Jax's spunk, enjoying the salty flavor of his lover. Then Jax withdrew his cock and walked around the horse until he was precisely where Lachlin wanted him to be. Lachlin was unable to prevent the sudden, unbidden image of when he and Jax had fucked Amaya in tandem, her face awash with pleasure, with Jax's beautiful face next to hers with his hunger present for all to witness. He groaned as the plug was turned off and removed.

He almost whimpered when he felt the head of Jax's cock against his ass. And then Jax thrust

21

forward, seating himself to the hilt in Lachlin's tight channel. Every nerve ending was set on fire at the delicious, almost violent feel of Jax's thrusts as he pounded inside him. Jax's fingers dug into Lachlin's hips. The slap of flesh mingled with Jax's moans, which he was no longer holding back.

One of Jax's hands gripped Lachlin's cock and squeezed as he hammered his channel ferociously. Lachlin's dick strained, enjoying the feel of Jax stroking and claiming him with his mastering.

"Come," Jax ordered.

Lachlin felt the orgasm start at the base of his spine. "Ahhh," he roared as hot streams jettisoned from his cock over the black leather of the horse.

Jax slammed inside him again, went rigid, and then Lachlin felt hot liquid fill his ass as Jax came. Jax thrust until every last drop had spilled into Lachlin's channel. Lachlin laid his face against the black leather as his own trembling subsided.

Jax unbound his hands and feet, helping him off the horse before they both collapsed in bed, not even caring about turning the sheets down. They lay side by side, staring at the ceiling.

Lachlin knew he had to broach the topic with him. It was only fair.

"Jax?" he asked, not looking at him. If the answer was no, Lachlin didn't want him to see his disappointment because then Jax would create all manner of insecure scenarios and Lachlin couldn't do that to him. He knew Jax's background, the desolate adolescence, and pain of growing up without a family. Jax rarely allowed anyone new into his life. Lachlin didn't blame him; he could understand his lover's reticence as Lachlin's upbringing mirrored Jax's.

"Hmmm?"

"You know what I would like?" Lachlin asked, his gut clenching.

"To challenge my recuperative powers and fuck again?"

"Well, that, and I want to entice Amaya to join us," he said. If Jax agreed, they could build from there. Once Lachlin could prove to him how amazing it would be to have a sub with them not just for the night, but for the long haul, Jax would allow it.

"Really? She was a hot piece, I will give you that. I wouldn't be averse to having her to fuck again for a night or two."

"I need this," Lachlin said.

Jax shot him a look. "If that's the case then bring her into our bed. Besides, it's only temporary. Pleasure Island is all about doing what you would never do elsewhere. If you want her to be our little plaything while we are here, I say let's do it. She did have a particularly juicy cunt if my memory serves correctly."

At Jax's easy acquiescence, Lachlin showed Jax just how appreciative he was and it was quite some time before they emerged from the villa.

They headed to the restaurant, Master's Pleasure, for some dinner before the club. While there was also a new pizza joint that was being run by the chef's youngest son, Michael, they had more than their fair share of pizza on the road. From what Lachlin had heard of Mrs. Davos' cooking, he was salivating at the thought of trying her fare.

The thirty or so tables in the restaurant were packed, putting the sound level at a dull roar. The main difference between Master's Pleasure and any other restaurant was that there was a good chance a Master could end up fucking his sub or disciplining them right at the table. At the thought of discipline, Lachlin felt a twinge in his ass. He still hadn't fully recovered from Jax's paddling and it would feel like he was sitting on hot coals for a day or so.

The restaurant reminded Lachlin of a gentlemen's pub in London. It was a bit sleeker but the dark, glossy woods and style made him wonder if they served brandy and cigars—after one had fucked their sub, of course. And bugger it all, there wasn't a single table available. The island had been in business now going into its second month. In the high end BDSM community, Doms and subs were flocking to the island getaway. Since Jared had officially started allowing guests from other high end clubs like the Dungeon Fantasy Club, he was apparently booked solid through Christmas. Luckily for them, Jared spied them as they were waiting near the hostess stand and waved them over.

"Why don't you join us?" Jared rose from his seat and shook their hands. "This is my Naomi," he went on, his voice laced with possession as he held his hand out to the pretty submissive wearing a skin tight, blue dress with a riot of dark curls framing her exotic face. She stood with Jared's assistance and gave Lachlin and Jax a once over before casting her gaze down.

"Pleasure to meet you, Naomi," Jax said, taking her hand, and giving her a buss on the back of her hand. *Just call him the Don Juan of flirtation.*

Lachlin did the same but with less flair. The last thing he wanted to do was piss Jared off by being too informal with his sub. "Pleasure, Naomi."

"Little one, these are Lachlin O'Toole and Jax Holiday, members of my club who tend to travel the world and never stay in one place."

"Hello, sirs. It's very nice to meet some of Jared's friends. You never told me that you had such good-looking friends. Maybe I've chosen the wrong Dom?" She shot a teasing gaze filled with merriment toward Jared, who in turn gave her a warning glance with enough heat behind it to start a forest fire.

"Careful, little one," Jared warned.

She rolled her eyes but then a blush spread over her cheeks. Lachlin almost laughed. Jared would make her pay for the eye-roll, and more, but he didn't think little Naomi would mind one bit.

They all sat, with Jax and Lachlin occupying the two empty chairs, and a knockout gorgeous waitress approached their table. "Master J, would your guests be interested in anything to eat tonight?"

"I know what I want to eat," Jax purred, laying it on thick. The blonde waitress was attractive if one liked big-breasted blondes. Lachlin preferred his little Japanese flower, Amaya, with her midnight hair that fell like a sheet to her mid-back and her luminous dark eyes. Jax's flirting didn't have the intended effect on the waitress; he might as well have been propositioning a newel post. Instead, she ignored the innuendo-laced comment, barely batting an eye, and listed the day's specials. Both he and Jax selected the flank steak with red wine burgundy sauce, steamed asparagus, and new potatoes. Lachlin didn't care for the waitress, Jenna. She was cold and detached.

"This place is great, J. Really, you have outdone yourself," Lachlin said, taking a sip of wine. The red was full-bodied and potent.

"Thank you. There are some further additions I would like to make but it's a start. How's the rest of the band?" Jared asked, leaning back in his seat, a hand resting on Naomi's exposed thigh.

"Well, you know that Bastian and Delilah are engaged."

"I'd heard that through the grapevine. I've been meaning to call and congratulate them. Declan mentioned that they are setting up shop together in Australia. I know Tyler and Elise are there with them, helping Bastian build a house on all the land he purchased a few years back. What are Collum and Eric up to? I'm surprised they didn't come with you."

Lachlin said, "Well, Collum headed home to Australia, too. He prefers spending his free time out in the Outback. Not what Bastian and Delilah have, on the very edges of civilization, but a bit more off the grid."

"Not that we have any clue as to why he prefers it. We grew up there. There's really not much to see," Jax interjected with a wave of his fork.

"And Eric?" Jared asked with a grin hovering on his face.

"He hooked up with this Swiss ski instructor at our last concert and they are currently in the Alps, skiing, among other things," Lachlin replied. He wasn't too concerned about his other band members. They always came back together when it was needed, but they did tend to scatter across the globe as soon as a tour finished. His curiosity was piqued regarding what Amaya was doing on the island, and he knew that Jared might have the inside scoop. The man seemed to know everyone's business.

"What's going on with the little violinist, Amaya? Know anything? She looked like someone had just kicked her puppy," Lachlin said.

Jared grimaced with a visible wince, then gave Lachlin an imperceptible glance. "I do know. Delilah called me. Someone was gunning for her seat with the London Symphony Orchestra, followed her to Castle Den in Amsterdam while the orchestra was touring there, and took pictures of her inside the club, which ended up getting her canned. She apparently had no idea she was being followed. Declan contacted The Dungeon to let the owner know that if they didn't improve their screening process, the DFC would pull their VIP Membership. So hopefully, any leaks in that club have been taken to task or fixed altogether."

Jax gave a low whistle.

Instantly sorry for what Amaya must be experiencing, Lachlin shook his head and said, "That's harsh. Bad deal all around."

"Yeah, well, Delilah mentioned that Amaya had some sort of fall-out with her family as well. She didn't know what because Amaya clammed up on that subject and, to be honest, I worry about saying the wrong thing. If I knew her better… Anyway, I'm going to have to intervene. During her first week here, she barely left her room. She hasn't set one foot in the club or used any of the facilities. All I know is that she leaves in the morning after breakfast and then comes back as the sun is setting. It's like she's become the island ghost. Why are you two so interested?"

Lachlin's heart ached for her. He knew now that he and Jax had to help her. "We met the sweet sub in Scotland and it's like she's had a personality change."

"Or a lobotomy," Jax muttered around a bite of steak.

"Jax," Lachlin said with an edge to his voice. The man at times was more dense than the Amazon rainforest.

Jax gave him a miffed glare and said, "What?"

Lachlin rolled his eyes. "Don't be a dick."

Jax's gaze hardened and judging by the fire blazing in his hazel eyes, he was incensed about Lachlin's words. Good. He needed to light a fire under his partner's ass. Lachlin needed this, even if he didn't understand the need fully. It wasn't like he wanted for companionship or felt neglected in the slightest by Jax, who was always ready. But Jax had been distracted of late as well. Maybe their road was coming to an end if Jax wouldn't cooperate, but Lachlin knew he had to help Amaya. That they had to rescue the poor girl.

"If you want some help, Jax and I have got this sub covered. We know her well enough that she might respond to us," Lachlin said, his heart aching for Amaya. He wanted to go stand sentinel outside her door and ensure that nothing harmed her further.

"In more ways than one," Jax interjected.

"Jax, there are days…" Lachlin shot him a glance.

"But you love me anyway."

"Be glad I do because no one else can handle you," Lachlin said with a derisive snort. How Jax could be so droll sometimes? A sub was in some serious trouble and all he did was make snarky comments.

Jared gave them both a relieved glance. "I'd be grateful. Normally, I would do something myself, but with Naomi's advent into my life I haven't found a replacement DM who isn't currently involved who could even attempt to breach her walls."

"We will see what we can do. We will try a soft attempt first, and if that fails…"

Jared reclined back in his seat. "If that fails, I will issue the command that to stay on the island, she must submit to you."

"Yeah, but I want to try my way first." Something told Lachlin that if they attempted to force a response from Amaya, she would lock her defenses up tighter than the crown jewels.

Her Music Masters

Chapter Three

The next morning, Amaya headed to what had become her private little spot on the island. It really was beautiful there. And peaceful. If she stared at the water long enough, its hypnotic waves lulled her into this complacent, safe space where she didn't think, didn't feel, and was just able to breathe.

Any time she reverted back to dwelling on her life, desolation settled in her soul. How had it come to this? A seagull arced across the blue sky. Waves crashed on their tumbling roll with the tide as it met the shoreline. She just could not fathom how her life had come to this when she'd worked so hard. She had all but killed herself to achieve perfection in pursuit of her dreams, to be the best in the world, and now, because someone had wanted to usurp her position in the orchestra, it had all been tossed in the trash. Amaya didn't even know how to begin fixing it. The magnitude of effort required to repair the damage was epic. And she didn't even know whether she had the energy to try.

Had the violin been her dream? Or had it been her parents' dream that she had super-imposed upon her life?

Amaya didn't know anymore. Whenever she poked at her emotions, to try and crack the shell around them, they poked back, almost suffocating her. If she opened herself up, it was going to hurt and she didn't think she would do anything but cry for days on end. Crying never solved a thing.

Amaya was staring at a point far off on the horizon. It looked like it was a cruise ship. When somebody unexpectedly sat beside her, she didn't jump. You have to feel alive to be able to be scared. As it was, she didn't feel anything.

She swiveled her head and spied Lachlin's bright blue eyes and disheveled, windblown blond hair. He'd forgotten to shave and there was a fine shadow beard, a shade darker than what was on his head, covering his jaw. She remembered nibbling on that jawline as his partner ate her pussy.

"Come here often?" Jax said to her as he sat beside her on her right.

She couldn't help herself and shot him a small smile. "To what do I owe the pleasure?"

Lachlin stroked a hand down her back, and all she wanted to do was lean into the comfort he so readily offered. "We missed you at the club last night," he murmured in his soothing, sexy baritone.

"Sorry. I was tired," she lied, because all she did was lie in bed and wonder what her next move should be, only to go around and around in circles until she was just as mired in confusion as she had been when she started. Amaya was no closer to a direction. How do you move forward when you have nothing left to lose?

33

"Understandable," Lachlin said, never once stopping his gentle caress over her back. Amaya felt a few of the knots in her shoulders begin to unwind. Without even realizing she was doing it, she did lean into him. The tender stroking was doing more for her than she realized, until she was practically crawling into his lap. This couldn't happen. She was too raw, too weak and needy. If she clung to him, what would that prove other than that she couldn't stand on her own?

When she started to move and withdraw, she found that Jax had closed in on her flank and had become a complete buffer. Both of them surrounded her on her little section of beach, shielding her from the world. She didn't relax so much as she burrowed into Lachlin's arms, soaking up all the heat of his body, even though it was a balmy ninety-five degrees.

They seemed to know precisely what it was that she needed. Tears didn't come. Amaya held the stopper on that with all her might. But she inhaled her first deep breath in forever, it seemed.

"Let it out, love," Lachlin murmured, placing a kiss on her brow as she burrowed.

"We're here for you," Jax said, resting his chin on her shoulder. It was strangely comforting. It wasn't like they knew each other all that well. Okay, so they had experienced an amazing night of sex way back when, but it wasn't like they had spilled all their deep dark secrets. It had been sex.

Really intense, she had been sore for days, incredible sex.

In the span of a few heartbeats, they had boxed her in to the point where she no longer thought of escape but wanted to know what she had to do to maintain the buffer and warmth they were providing her. How had they so totally disarmed her so quickly? Sneaky Doms. Was she an easy mark?

"We know about it, love, Jared filled us in. It will be all right," Lachlin whispered against her brow and her gut clenched.

She'd never told Jared about what had happened. Granted, there had been mention made in one of the London newspapers, saying that she had been replaced. Amaya could only assume that Delilah had called Jared. She was the one who had suggested this resort in the first place. Which just proved how not in her right mind Amaya was. Once she had more energy, she'd call Delilah and give her an earful. Amaya knew her friend had done it out of love and concern but it was her life, and her story, as screwed up as it may be.

"You don't know everything. And no, it will never be all right again." A haggard breath expelled from her lungs. Because she hadn't told Delilah what her father had said and done. That he had cut all ties with her and expressly forbidden the rest of her family from contacting her. It meant she'd lost her mother, her grandmother, her aunt, and her cousins, all in one fell swoop. Her father was the patriarch of the family. What he commanded was as good as law in her family.

Lachlin cupped her cheek, turning her face up toward his. The intensity of his gaze wriggled inside her foggy responses, and Amaya felt a hum of desire ignite. It wasn't much of a spark but she held on to that shiny, warm flame with everything left inside of her.

"Why don't you come back to our villa and let us take care of you, love?" Lachlin suggested.

"Why?" she asked.

"Because we would like to repeat the fabulous sex we had in Scotland," Jax said, one of his hands toying with the exposed skin on her lower back, teasing the waistband of her jeans.

"Jax," Lachlin growled, and it almost made her smile. "We would like you to be our sub while we are here on the island," he explained.

As much as she tried to come up with an excuse to say no in her overwrought brain, she couldn't. Jax was correct in that the sex between the three of them had been off the chain. And her body all but liquefied at their touch. Her brain might be on vacation and her heart and soul weren't speaking to her, but her body's response to being surrounded by them was a lifeline she couldn't turn away from. Her current funk was something she had no idea how to conquer or overcome.

Amaya groaned and her eyes slid shut as Lachlin's clever mouth took hers in a heart-stopping kiss. He knew just how to kiss her. He seduced with butterfly kisses, his hands softly cupping her face, creating the sensation that she was precious to him. It stirred her. After going so long without feeling anything but despair, she gave herself over to his gentle possession. Jax's hands cupped her breasts and he nibbled on her exposed shoulder.

It wasn't the firestorm it had been before, but Amaya wasn't right in the head presently, and knew it was all her. Maybe if she allowed it and said yes, she could find her way back. What else did she have to lose?

Nothing. Not a god damn thing.

Jax bit down on her shoulder, harder this time, sending sparks of electricity shooting through her veins. At the growing intensity of pleasure, she made her decision and she gasped. "Yes. I will."

Lachlin released her lips and pulled back, giving her a gentle smile, running his thumb over her bottom lip. "Good. Why don't we get you home and we can begin?"

She nodded her head in agreement.

Jax pinched her nipples through her shirt and she yelped at the strains of fire that sailed directly to her sex, which throbbed in response. Then he said, "Or we could just start here? I know I'm ready."

"Jax. You're always ready. I prefer not to get sand up my ass. Let's go," Lachlin said.

"I could make you, but I will play nice today," Jax replied with a hint of steel behind his voice.

Lachlin rolled his eyes at him and said, "It's about damn time."

"You'll pay for that."

"I always do," Lachlin muttered as he lifted her off his lap and stood. Then he helped her stand and she swayed. She enjoyed their banter. Amaya would have laughed if she'd had the energy.

"Christ, when was the last time you had anything to eat?" Lachlin said, scooping her up in his arms like she didn't weigh a thing.

"I don't remember." She had just pushed her food around on her plate this morning. And last night, after a few bites, she'd lost her appetite.

"Well, we'll fix that as well. You will be staying with us for the next two weeks. As soon as we are at the villa, I will contact Jared and have your things brought over."

"Okay." She didn't have the heart to argue with him. She didn't really have a heart anymore. The pieces of it lay scattered on the ground where her father had shattered it.

She turned her face into his shoulder and shut her eyes. Deep down, she didn't believe anyone could help her. It was sweet that Lachlin wanted to try. Jax was just along for the ride, but

Lachlin, he seemed to see inside her soul and know just how to touch her and invade her space.

Had she made the right decision? Or would putting her fate in their hands make whatever life she had left tumble into the sea?

Chapter Four

Lachlin was concerned about Amaya's tepid response. This woman had been all fire during their first encounter months ago. And yet, as she clung to him, he held her tighter, wanting to defeat whatever darkness she faced and be her bastion against it.

Jared had been correct to assume something was wrong. It was worse than Lachlin had first thought. Every square inch of the Dom inside him was ready to slay every one of her demons, or help her do it, at the very least. He glanced at Jax as he drove them back to their villa, and there was a light in Jax's eyes that he recognized well. Jax had morphed into his protective alpha Dom mode, and Lachlin loved him all the more for it.

It took them less than ten minutes to motor back to the villa but with each passing moment, Lachlin became more resolved than ever to help the trembling woman in his arms. He carried her into the elevator and then into their room. She was like a rag doll. Her responses to stimuli were dull. She didn't comment on the room or ask any questions.

They had to tread carefully, otherwise they would make it worse. He held her like she was porcelain.

Once they were safely ensconced within the villa, Lachlin sat on the couch, keeping her nestled in his arms, feeling the whipcord tension in her body. Jax sat beside him. Putting her feet in his lap, Jax removed her sandals, then began stroking her feet.

"Since you are going to be with us for a bit, do you have any hard limits we need to know about?" Lachlin asked, caressing her legs, her back, trying to ease the duress in her slight form.

She didn't look at him or at Jax, just mumbled into his chest. "Umm, I'm not a fan of medical play and I'm not a pain slut."

Jax leaned in. "And what's your stance on watching me fuck Lachlin?"

"Um, that doesn't bother me." Even her voice was lifeless.

Jax pressed her as he continued to rub her feet. "Does it turn you on?" he asked.

"I think so. Maybe. I'm sorry, I don't know," she said.

Jax asked, "Search your feelings, what does your body tell you?"

Amaya cringed against him and Lachlin shot Jax a murderous glance. "I don't know. Maybe you should find another sub who isn't so messed up. I'm no good. I'm no good for anyone."

Oh, baby. Lachlin's heart broke for her. Whatever had occurred with her family had scarred her deeply. He wanted to make all her hurts go away.

She trembled in his arms. Amaya was like a dam on the verge of breaking. If she didn't relieve the pressure, and soon, she was going to blow and it would be cataclysmic. At her pitiful response, Jax, ever the warrior, morphed into an over-protective Dom.

"Why do you say you're no good?" Jax pressed, his hazel gaze intently focused on every gesture Amaya made in Lachlin's arms.

She shrugged. "I'm just not."

Jax pushed her further than Lachlin felt comfortable with and said, "Amaya, if you are going to be with us, we do want honesty from you. You know you cannot have a good relationship with a Dom, let alone two, if you aren't honest with us."

"But I am being honest. I can't seem to feel anything anymore. I think it's because I'm not good for anyone. I'm useless, and—"

"Stop," Lachlin said, much more harshly than he had intended and felt her tense in his arms.

"I'm sorry, Sir." Her breath hitched. She was breaking his heart. Lachlin shot a glance at Jax and they communicated silently. Sex was off the table for the time being. She was so much more wounded than he had originally suspected.

They would have sex eventually, but his and Jax's first responsibility was to her entire well-being. Right now, it wasn't sex. It couldn't be losing her job which had put her in this state. It had to be whatever had happened with her family. They would get to the bottom of it and help this little sub heal her broken soul. One way or the other. Lachlin made it his mission to see her through the darkness to whatever end. It was no longer about what he wanted or desired in adding a female sub to the mix, it was about saving the beauty with haunted eyes in his arms.

Jax scooted out from under her feet, placing them tenderly on the couch, then rose and headed into the bathroom. A nice hot bubble bath was what the doctor ordered. She needed to feel safe, she needed to feel protected, and she needed a landing spot so that she could fall apart.

When he heard the water running, Lachlin stood, still cradling her in his arms, and headed to the bathroom. Jax was already disrobing when they entered. Lachlin set her on the lip of the tub and began helping her out of her clothes. He was concerned by how listless she seemed. It barely registered that he was stripping her down.

When he had removed every stitch of clothing and she sat there naked, quaking, with her arms around her midsection as he disrobed, Lachlin knew that drastic measures were needed. He wasted no time in removing his clothes, not minding where they fell. Then he climbed into the tub. He sat and then Jax helped move her into the tub with him. It was large enough that it could seat four people comfortably.

Lachlin gathered her close as Jax entered the tub on the other end and sat opposite them. Jax inched forward until he was seated between Lachlin's knees, then he positioned his legs, bent at the knee, over his legs. Lachlin fit Amaya between them. They were going to completely cocoon her. Lachlin bore the brunt of her weight, and had her lean her back against his chest. The bubbles teased them with glimpses of her nipples and the shaved juncture between her thighs. They were going to use the jets to soothe her and hopefully draw her out of her shell a bit. She was still stiff in his arms. Then Jax placed her legs on either side of his waist.

They soothed her. Lachlin began with her neck and shoulders, kneading the taut flesh, while Jax started on her calves. She moaned but it wasn't the response Lachlin wanted. They needed to crack her defenses, make her become familiar with their touch, and learn to trust them implicitly. Only then would they be able to help her heal. There was not an inch of her body their hands did not touch. Lachlin couldn't help himself as he tasted her neck with his tongue. She was far too tempting a morsel and he had to fight back his own raging lust. His hands learned the contours of her breasts, enjoying the small but firm buds, and at the way her nipple pebbled beneath his touch, he bit back a groan. He wanted to indulge himself and feast on her body. He couldn't wait to see the tiny orbs wearing clamps, or to suck the tiny bud into his mouth.

44

Jax caressed her labia, running his fingers through her slit. And Lachlin could tell Jax wanted to fuck her from the size of his erection poking up through the bubbles. His own cock was just as hard. And feeling her firm ass against his shaft was nearly driving him wild. They would both fuck her, more than once, but they needed to heal her first. Her current responses were far too tepid. The way Jax was playing with her pussy, she should be writhing with unrepentant need. As it was, she was barely thrusting her hips, it was more of an ingrained response.

Lachlin sucked her earlobe into his mouth and bit down slightly. She moaned, undulating her hips as Jax teased her slit. And still she held back.

"Let go, Amaya, tell us what hurts and we will help," he whispered.

She seized up in his arms, going from pliant to rigid in a millisecond.

Fuck, the only way they were going to get any answers from her was in sub space. She'd locked herself up tighter than a maximum-security prison. They couldn't risk spanking or anything that walked the line of punishment. In the state she was in, they could push her further over the edge and that would do the opposite of what they intended.

He had an idea. But he wasn't certain how Jax would take it.

"Let's get you into bed, sweetheart." He kissed her temple.

Jax climbed out of the tub first and grabbed a towel. Once they were all dry, Lachlin said, "Why don't you go climb into bed and we'll be with you in a minute."

"Yes, Sir, whatever you want."

The moment she left the bathroom, he turned to Jax and said, "I have an idea."

"Good, because I don't and frankly, I'm not sure we can help her," Jax said, shaking his head in frustration.

"We have to try." Lachlin couldn't get past the thought that if anyone could help her, it was the two of them.

"What's your idea?" Jax asked, and Lachlin filled him in on the angle he wanted to pursue.

"It could work. We will try that route for now. If it fails, we will have to figure out something else. Maybe she does need the pain of a good spanking to break through her walls." Jax stroked his chin as he contemplated the idea.

"Maybe, but I don't think so. I think this will work. You up for it?"

"I sure hope she really is what you want, Lachlin, because we are going to a lot of trouble here," Jax said.

Lachlin hoped so, too.

*****

Amaya curled into a ball on the bed. She was failing, even at being a submissive. How could she be messing this up? Before the cataclysm that destroyed her life, she had excelled at being a submissive. Except, in this instance, she was letting these two wonderful Doms down and she didn't know what to do. Lachlin had been so kind to her. When they had been together in Scotland, there had been a potent connection between them that was almost soul deep. She would do anything to feel that way again.

She was hopeless.

"Lie on your back for us, sweetheart," Lachlin ordered, the command inherent behind his words.

She did as he bade. This was something she could do; she could follow orders. Everything else, she would try and give it her all.

"Give us your hands," Jax commanded as both Doms flanked the sides of the bed. It wasn't lost on her that they both were sporting erections. Their cocks jutted from their taut bellies.

She lifted her arms as they fitted her wrists into Velcro restraints. Then they did the same with her ankles so that she was spread-eagled on the bed. The ankle restraints had more leeway in their length, which made it possible for the Doms to bend her knees if they wanted to.

"Now, we are going to play a little game. For every question you answer, you get an orgasm. For every delay tactic, you will not be permitted to climax until we allow it. Do you understand?"

47

Anya Summers

Lachlin said, looking every inch a Dom with Jax
flanking him.

She swiveled her gaze between both men.
They weren't going to allow her to hide her hurts
away. As much as she knew deep down that she
needed their help, she had prided herself on being
able to go it alone and handle everything herself.

"Amaya," Lachlin said, with a hint of
frustration lacing his voice.

"Yes, Sirs. I will try."

Her response seemed to appease him and he
gave her a dazzling smile. "That's all we ask for,
sweetheart. Your safeword is 'red,' but I don't think
you will need it."

The mattress sank and shifted under their
combined weight as they climbed into bed beside
her. The intent to seduce was clearly written on
their faces. The muscles in her abdomen tightened
and a little shiver coursed down her spine. She just
had to remember to breathe. She wasn't facing a
firing squad. Although it was no less daunting.

They lay beside her, one on either side.
They took turns kissing her. Lachlin's kiss was one
she sank into, moving her lips with his as he
seduced. His kisses were a drug to her senses and
she fell under his spell with every gentle caress.
And then he released her and Jax shifted her face
toward his. Where Lachlin's kisses were like a lazy
Sunday morning, Jax was an atom bomb to her
system. He didn't barter or beg, he plundered her

defenses until her head swam and she was awash in him as he plumbed her depths.

Back and forth, they each took turns kissing her to the point where she began to crave the differences in their kiss. Each one was more heady than the last. And then they kissed her together, their tongues sliding in her mouth, teasing the corners of her lips, and stroking their tongues against one another. Flames ignited in her belly and seeped into her core. It was as if her body had been sleepwalking through her life, and now their touch had awakened her body. She wanted more, wanted to feel more of their delicious kisses. If they could just do this all day...

They whet her appetite, stoking the fires she had believed were dormant and at times no longer existed. Their cocks rested against her hips, their shafts erect, and her core fluttered in anticipation. Would they fuck her like they had in Scotland? Double penetrating her, make her delirious with need as they screwed her brains out?

Then they broke their triad kiss.

"What happened at work? Why did they fire you?" Lachlin asked, his fingers caressing the slope of her breast. It was like a whisper as his fingers barely touched and it made her shiver.

Jax closed his lips around her nipple, tugging the tip greedily into his mouth and Amaya gasped at the unexpected pleasure spiking through her body.

"It was one of the second stringers, Edward Walsh. He had been gunning for my spot for a while, but he can't play a diminished ninth to save his soul."

Jax bit down on her engorged nipple and like a livewire it sent shockwaves straight to her pussy. Then he released the swollen nub, laving it with his tongue before suckling the pert bud back into his mouth. She wanted to feed him her breast to make the delicious pleasure never end. This was the best she had felt in weeks.

Lachlin interrupted her pleasure buzz and asked another question. "And he was the one who took pictures of you at the club?"

"Yes," she hissed as Jax did a series of nibbling bites against her nipple and waves of pleasure deluged her system. She wished that she could hold him there at her breast.

"Did you know he was taking pictures of you?"

"No, I—um, oh, god," she moaned. Jax and Lachlin's fingers were both stroking through her crease and it was a little slice of heaven. It was the most alive she'd felt in weeks. If they could just keep doing it...

"Amaya." Their fingers stilled and she had to think of her response. Had she known Edward was filming her, taking pictures of her? No, she hadn't.

"Um, no, I didn't," she replied.

"Why didn't any of the DMs at the club stop him?" Lachlin asked.

That made Amaya still. Why hadn't any of them? She had never even considered that they should have stopped it. She had just been so startled about getting fired. The conductor had tossed the photos in her face; pictures of her up on a St. Andrew's Cross being whipped. It was a shock that he had seen them and the disgust that had been on his face would live with her forever. But she had never considered how Edward was able to procure the photos. Castle Den didn't allow cell phones or cameras into the main den. The Doms and subs all had lockers to put their things into.

"I don't know. Castle Den, the dungeon monitors have always been good to me." Or at least they had, but had something more been going on? Had she pissed off a Dom at the club and he had helped Edward get the photos? You had to be a member to enter the Den. Then her eyes almost crossed as Jax and Lachlin's hands stroked her pussy.

"Well, someone failed at their job, Amaya. That wasn't your fault. Do you think Jared would allow someone to film a sub unknowingly in his club?"

Their hands stilled and she whined. Would Jared allow something like that? She shook her head and said, "No. He would toss them out on their ass."

51

"Precisely, love. What happened wasn't your fault," Lachlin said as Jax moved his full body between her thighs. She watched his dark head descend as he replaced his fingers on her clit with his mouth. His tongue swiped through her slit, from her clit all the way to her back rosette. She undulated her hips against his mouth before his hands clamped down on them. Jax proved that they were in control of when she climaxed. If the torture weren't so wonderful, she'd be screaming for release. As it was, she just wanted to float and swim in this pleasure-filled cornucopia.

"I want you to say it," Lachlin demanded, rolling a nipple between his thumb and forefinger. Pleasure pain zinged all the way to her core and momentarily stole her breath.

Jax stopped flicking his tongue against her clit. If their intent was to drive her crazy with need, it was working.

"It wasn't my fault," she said, mumbling, because as much as her mind was coming around to their way of thinking, her heart and soul were another matter entirely.

"Again," Lachlin demanded.

"It wasn't my fault," she said, louder this time, and then she was rewarded as Jax feasted on her pussy once more.

"Oh god," she moaned as her body tightened in on itself.

Lachlin pinched her nipples and they swelled under his ministrations. "Why do you think you aren't any good, that you don't deserve anything good and decent?"

Jax bit down on her clit, sending volts of lightning throughout her body as her pleasure built. She was so close to the promised orgasm. Her body was awakening as if from a deep sleep. But then he stopped and she whimpered.

"Because I lost everything that day." Her breath hitched in the back of her throat. Her landlord in London had evicted her when someone had pasted the graphic pictures of her throughout the apartment building. And then she had gone limping home back to Japan, the one place where she thought she could hide away from the rest of the world to make her move, but Edward had mailed a copy of the pictures to her parents' home. Her father had turned her away at the door.

Jax gave her clit a series of fast flicks with his tongue and stopped. "What did you lose?"

"My career, my home, my family." Her breath hitched again and between one breath and the next, the dam she'd been plugging disintegrated into dust. One moment she was on the verge of climax, and in the next, her tears were falling fast and furious.

"Red, red, red!" she wailed. She strained against the Velcro straps, wanting to curl into herself. She sobbed, blinded by her tears, her panic rising that she couldn't hide her pain from them. Her great, heaving sobs were loud even to her ears. She felt like she had been turned inside out.

Lachlin and Jax removed her restraints, attempting to soothe her with their calm touch. Then they gathered her close, one man on each side. They did nothing but hold her, surrounding her with their strength as she emptied her grief. She cried until her eyes were swollen from the tears and her body exhausted.

Amaya finally drifted off as the worst of the storm battering her defenses subsided, safe in the knowledge that Lachlin and Jax were there.

*****

Amaya cracked her eyes open when she heard a deep-throated male moan beside her. She looked over and a ball of lust enveloped her. Jax lay on his back as Lachlin gave him head. It was one of the most erotic things she had ever witnessed. Her body revved back to life and her pussy throbbed.

She shifted her body, rolling on to her side so that she could watch the show. It alerted both men to the fact that she was awake. Jax gave her a sideways glance as Lachlin released his cock.

Jax said, "I didn't tell you that you could stop. Continue, or I'll fuck her ass instead and leave you begging for my cock." Then he said to Amaya, "How do you feel, sweetheart? We didn't mean to wake you but I was getting a case of blue balls after sucking your juicy pussy."

Heat spread through her cheeks and wetness trickled down her thighs. "I feel good." And she meant it. She had needed that crying jag more than she realized. She felt calm, less like a pressure cooker about to explode. She wasn't necessarily happy but she noticed how much more alive she felt, like she was no longer walking through fog.

"I'm glad." Jax stroked a knuckle down her cheek. "Now, how about you put that pretty pussy of yours over my mouth so I can finish the job I started? I don't like leaving things undone."

She moaned in the back of her throat and said, "Yes, Sir."

With his help, she straddled his face so that her pussy hovered above his mouth. He said, "Play with your tits while I suck your sweet cunt." Then his tongue swiped against her hood. Her back bowed as her hands cupped her breasts. She tugged the nipples between her fingers, rolling the peaks.

Jax did not hold back this time, bringing her body back to where he had left off in no time. The man was a General in the erotic and on a campaign to make her climax. His tongue plunged inside her channel, mercilessly stroking all her sensitive places. Amaya's moans mixed with the wet sounds of Lachlin sucking Jax's cock. The musk of their sex spiced the air. Jax held her in place as he plundered, his fingers digging into her hips, humming in the back of his throat as he slurped at her dew. He also used his teeth, biting down on her swollen clit. Pleasure pulsated through her body at the sharp pleasure pain. And then he thrust his tongue inside her drenched channel once more and Amaya couldn't stop the series of mewls as they erupted from her mouth. He smacked her ass cheek and she keened. He did it a second time, her pussy clenched around his tongue, and the sparkling cliff of her release neared. The next swat sent her body over the edge. She arched back as her body compressed around his tongue and she exploded.

"Oh," she wailed as tremors wracked her body, trembling and writhing against his mouth, feeling moisture flow down her thighs. Then it was his turn to moan. His fingers dug into her thighs as he trumpeted his release, his hips bucking as he spewed inside Lachlin's mouth. He suckled her tiny swollen nub as he came, sparking another series of spasms that made her grip the headboard.

Then, with Lachlin's help, she climbed off Jax's face, her thighs trembling at the forced movement and she collapsed on her back, her body still on the hazy plane of afterglow. Jax lay supine beside her as he caught his breath.

"It's my turn," Lachlin said, crawling over to her and nudging her thighs apart. Then his mouth claimed her pussy and all she could do was groan. Jax rolled to his side, his hand teased her breast and he kissed her. It was a delicious, sensual mingling of lips and tongue meant to drive her body right back up the cliff of desire. She could taste herself on Jax's lips, all while Lachlin paid homage to her pussy. He all but worshiped her flesh with his tongue, eating her pussy like it was a rare delicacy that he wanted to savor.

Amaya moaned into Jax's mouth as a wave of desire swept through her system. She was sliding back into a pleasure-filled haze and she wanted to gorge on it. And then Jax released her lips. She whimpered at the loss of his mouth as he rolled off the bed. Where was he going? Then Lachlin flicked his tongue against her clit in a series of fast strokes and her mouth fell open on what seemed like a continual moan. Amaya yearned to be filled with something other than just Lachlin's wonderful tongue. It was driving her crazy but she needed something thicker, fuller, and longer than his tongue. She needed his cock.

"Please, Sir," she whined, attempting to undulate her hips but he wouldn't allow it. Lachlin was in complete control of her pleasure and whether he would allow her to have more or not. Amaya was at the point where she was willing to beg. He raised his golden head up, his chin coated with her juices.

"Please what?"

"Please. I need you to fuck me, Sir."

"That's more like it." He crawled up her body, nudging her thighs further apart to accommodate the width of his hips and she welcomed the feeling. It meant she would soon feel his glorious cock inside her.

Jax came up behind Lachlin sporting a proud erection. The duo looked like fierce Spartan warriors, confident in their manhood, unabashed about their naked bodies. She licked her lips at the sight of their bulging shafts. Jax rolled a condom over Lachlin's rigid cock and then, still holding his lover's dick, drew it down, stroking it through Amaya's folds. Jax bit Lachlin's shoulder as he fit Lachlin's cock at the entrance to her sheath. "Fuck her, Lachlin, while I fuck you."

On a groan, Lachlin thrust his hips and penetrated her to the hilt. He filled her, her body suffused and overflowing with his shaft. As she adjusted to his extra-long length, taking him all the way to the hilt, her body craved movement, needing him to fuck her. But Lachlin didn't move and stilled, embedded deep inside her pussy. She writhed a bit under him, moaning her frustration.

"Hold still for just a moment, Amaya, and then I promise to fuck you until you can't walk," Lachlin ordered.

"Promises, promises," she said, getting impatient. He pussy throbbed around his cock. Then she watched Lachlin's face contort into ecstasy as Jax thrust into his ass.

"Remind me to spank her, after we've fucked her, for her impudent mouth," Jax said.

58

"Yes, Sir," Lachlin replied on a groan. And then they moved as one, plunging and withdrawing almost in sync.

Amaya met their combined thrusts with her own. It was like nothing she had ever experienced. It was like they were both fucking her as they thrust together. Lachlin gripped her tight, burying his face in her neck. She wrapped her arms around his back, riding the force of their lovemaking. Lachlin's firm length slid against her nerve endings with each stroke. It was bliss, feeling his cock plunder inside her, hitting the lip of her womb. She couldn't remember ever feeling so complete. She never wanted the pounding thrusts to stop. Over and over, she undulated her hips as Lachlin slammed inside her pussy. Her walls gripped his cock, trying to draw him deeper. Lachlin grunted as Jax's pace increased as he pummeled his ass. The slap of flesh and the heady musk of their sex filled the room. Jax leaned forward, supporting himself on his hands as he thrust deeper inside Lachlin.

It was incredible. She'd had lovers aplenty, but this was on another level entirely. Having Jax's intent, lust-filled face so near hers while Lachlin's was buried at her neck, his grumbling moans filling her ears, was erotic. It drove her own desire higher up the mountain.

It was like they had no end and no beginning. But Jax tapped Lachlin on the shoulder and then both men stopped.

Amaya wailed. She wanted, *needed* to come and they weren't letting her. "Sirs, please?"

"Not yet, pet," Jax said. She watched him insert an extra-large butt plug into Lachlin's ass. Lachlin gripped her tightly as the plug slid home, mumbling nearly incoherently into her neck. Jax turned the vibrating feature of the plug on and Lachlin groaned so deep and loud, his cock elongating inside her clasping sheath, she was surprised he didn't blow his load then and there.

"Lie on your back and fuck her, Lachlin. I want to take that tight rosette," Jax commanded.

They were going to double penetrate her. Just like that first time in Scotland.

Her body shook as Lachlin helped Jax rearrange her so that she was straddling Lachlin's hips. She rose on her knees as he fitted his crown at her entrance. Then he plunged inside and she was keening, her sex gripping him, trying to pull him deeper. But then Jax was behind her, bending her forward until her face was an inch from Lachlin's. As his hungry blue gaze bored into hers, need swirled. Lachlin closed the gap and took her lips in a devastating kiss as Jax slathered her anus with lube. He pushed a finger inside, past the tight ring of muscle and she exhaled in Lachlin's mouth as he continued kissing her until she saw stars behind her lids. Jax worked in first one finger, then two, until they were gliding through her tissues with ease. And then he fit the fat head of his cock at her back hole. Lachlin withdrew from her pussy as Jax worked his cock into her ass.

Pleasure pain zinged her system as he thrust and retreated, stretching her back channel until he was able to seat himself all the way in. She dug her fingers into Lachlin's chest. When Jax was fully embedded in her ass, he stopped moving, and only then did Lachlin penetrate her pussy. It was almost too much, the feel of them both inside her. Jax filling her ass made her pussy tighter as Lachlin slid home. She was overflowing, so full it made her realize how empty her life had been. She dug her fingers into Lachlin's firm chest. She couldn't move, couldn't do anything but feel. She was suffused with their cocks and it was glorious. All her nerve endings were ablaze and she wanted— nay, she needed—more friction. She panted as her desire rose.

"Sirs," she whined.

And then they withdrew until only the heads of their cocks remained inside before driving them back inside her. She saw stars behind her closed lids. She started babbling and had no idea what she was saying. She just wanted them to keep on fucking her. Something she said must have made them unleash their primitive sides, because one minute they were casually fucking her and the next, they were fucking her with a fury that stole all rational thought processes from her mind. Amaya turned into a mass of need as their cocks hammered inside her.

Over and over, they pounded her system. As their control began to slip, both men were jack-hammering inside her with their own rhythm, not bothering to keep in sync with their partner. She was never without a cock plunging inside her. The best was when they did sync up and plowed inside her sheaths at the same time. Her body coiled in on itself, and Amaya felt like she had been moaning continually forever. She couldn't stop moaning as her body tightened, straining toward release. Between one thrust and the next, her body splintered and shattered.

"Oh, god!" she screamed as her body shuddered and quaked, but they kept on fucking her, taking her body to new heights. Only when they had made her come twice more did they let go and find their own release.

Her body fluttered and clenched around them as she detonated into a million pieces.

Chapter Five

Amaya awoke the next day just as dawn was streaking the horizon. Lachlin and Jax were still snoring away. They were both gorgeous men in their own right. Lachlin looked like an angel with his halo of golden hair and blue eyes and when she looked at his body, she felt her face flame. Ripcord lean and lanky, everything on him was huge—from his hands to his feet, and everything in between. It was nearly a religious experience to be the sole focus of his attention. The memory made her limbs liquefy and her sex throb.

Her head swiveled to the right. And then there was the sinfully delicious Jax. A bit of a rogue, he was dark where Lachlin was light. A wealth of pitch-black short hair crowned his head and gave the appearance that he ran his fingers through it a million times a day. He wasn't as tall as Lachlin, but his chest was even more muscular, and he had veritable tree trunks for arms and legs. And then there was his cock… her face flamed even hotter. Holy smokes, it was so wide and thick, penetration walked the line of pain. He wasn't as long as Lachlin, only about seven inches, but his girth was larger than her fist and she felt every blissful inch of him.

Her body yearned to feel them, to be with them, to submit to whatever wicked delights they could possibly contrive. And that hit her internal panic button. Her heart rate accelerated and she found she was shaking.

Before she woke them up, whereupon they would try and persuade her from doing what she knew she had to do, she slipped quietly from the bed. Last night had been wonderful. She enjoyed being with them, perhaps a little too much. Her heart trembled. Amaya wasn't ready to get involved, not when her life was as unsettled as it was. They had given her a gift yesterday in helping her release some of her sorrow. It would be a memory that she would pull out and relive when the tide of her life became too much. Because of their loving, she felt more like herself than she had done since her world disintegrated. But this was where it had to end.

She couldn't allow herself to depend upon them. What would happen to her if she allowed herself to need them? They were like an addictive drug to her system. In her current state, she worried about permitting them inside her heart only to have them toss her away. Her family, the people who were supposed to love her without question, seemed to have no problem cutting her out of their lives. Neither Lachlin nor Jax had mentioned that they wanted anything beyond a mere dalliance while they were all on the island. And she just couldn't do it.

It was too risky a venture for Amaya to allow the liaison to continue, even as her body warred with her decision to leave, craving their deft touches and lovemaking with a ferocity that scared her. A part of her yearned to climb back into bed and snuggle, and then maybe wake them both for another round. Instead of giving in to the decadent temptation they presented, as quietly as she could, she tiptoed out into the living room, where her luggage had been delivered, and got dressed. She could feel the depression swamping her system. Not having a family to turn to anymore, coupled with her father's last words, which seemed to play on a recorded loop in her brain, brought about an unending tide of grief that swallowed her whole into a pit of despair when she least expected it. It was all too much. And she couldn't stay here.

She grabbed a bottle of water and a banana on her way toward the door, putting them in the small knapsack she always carried while traveling. Her mahogany wood violin case rested on one of the chairs. Seeing it there, an unholy rage settled in her soul. That thing had caused her nothing but pain. As quietly as she dared, she located a box of matches and charcoal lighter fluid in one of the kitchen drawers. It was designed for the bar-b-que pit out on the deck, but she had another idea for its use in mind. Putting everything in her pack, she slung it over her shoulder and picked up her violin on her way out the door. With a last glance at the two sleeping forms, her heart breaking just a little bit more, she angrily swiped at the fresh bout of tears leaking from her eyes and silently closed the door behind her.

By the time Amaya walked onto the path heading toward her secluded beach, the sun had fully crested the horizon. Birds sang sweetly as she marched. She needed to put distance between herself and temptation, and she gripped the handle of her case tighter. Little geckos scurried across the ground. In her heart, she was resolved about her next course of action. It was time she had a full break with her past, starting with her violin. And then she'd figure out a way to make a break in her heart with her family. She didn't have a family anymore. She wasn't enough for them, and couldn't fathom why they couldn't seem to love her for who she was, not who they wanted her to be.

If her family, the ones who were supposed to love her without question, couldn't stomach who she was, she was a fool for even hoping that anyone else would.

The unfairness of it all blazed within her soul as her rage seethed.

*****

Lachlin shook his partner awake and Jax cast him a one-eyed, bleary gaze, refusing to open both. Jax was not a morning person in any way, shape or form. Disturbing him while he was sleeping was risking bodily injury.

"What? Unless you plan to suck my dick, leave me alone and let me sleep," Jax growled, reaching for the covers to pull them back over his head.

"Amaya's gone," Lachlin said, panic evident in his voice.

Dammit. This little sub was turning out to be far more trouble than her sweet cunt was worth. Jax knew Lachlin wanted her, for reasons he hadn't begun to fathom. "So?" he mumbled as he stretched. He liked her, he did, but in less than twenty-four hours, she'd already been the mother of all headaches. That didn't mean he hadn't enjoyed the sweet taste of her honeyed nectar or the tight clasp of her rosette around his dick. But for fuck's sake, he was here to relax and have a good time, not deal with a problematic sub.

It was why he had never suggested adding anyone to his relationship with Lachlin. He liked what they had together, and didn't want anything to change.

Lachlin gave him a patronizing glare and said, "Dude, don't be an ass. You saw her last night. She needs us."

She needed something, but Jax wasn't certain that it was them. Maybe what she needed was a professional who could help her navigate whatever the hell it was she was dealing with, someone with a license who could prescribe medication if need be. Except Jax realized by the sheer determination in Lachlin's earnest gaze that he wasn't going to allow him to get any more sleep until the little violinist was located. Jax sat up in bed, feeling a burr up his butt over the entire situation. "Are you sure it's not you needing her? Maybe she doesn't want to be found and we should leave well enough alone, man."

Lachlin looked like he wanted to shake some sense into him. Jax loved him. They had been friends in the orphanage from the time they were eight, and lovers since they were twenty-two, but lately it worried him that Lachlin seemed to be seeking fulfillment outside their relationship. Lachlin was intent on adding a woman and making their duo a permanent threesome. It wasn't that Jax was appalled by the idea. Hell, he liked fucking a woman just as much as the next guy. But it seemed to be something that Lachlin was searching for, and that was an issue Jax had attempted to shy away from and ignore.

It didn't appear as though that was going to work anymore. Lachlin wanted Amaya. And Jax did feel sorry for the little sub—he felt for her, period. It was clear she'd been through a hell of a time and was floundering. As a Dom, it was his sacred duty to help a drowning submissive if he could. He wondered if he and Lachlin were the right ones to accomplish it, though. She needed a gentle guiding hand, which was not his strong suit. He enjoyed storming the defenses and forcing a

68

surrender. That wasn't what she needed and it made him uneasy because he wasn't certain he wouldn't fail her.

"Be that as it may, Jax, I consider her our sub while we are here and if you plan on being a piss-poor Dom, then I can bunk with Amaya in her room at the hotel." Lachlin's rigid determination, and apparent willingness to put their relationship aside to assist the sub, stoked fear in Jax.

"Hold up, where is this coming from? If you are unhappy and want out, just say so." Jax tensed, ready for the end. It was a knee-jerk response, due to their upbringing. But he had been in the orphanage longer than Lachlin. He had separation issues that ran deeper. Lachlin's parents had died in a house fire, not Jax's. His had deserted him when he was six. They had left him home alone one day and never come back. It was a neighbor who had noticed he was all by himself and gotten the authorities involved. It was why he didn't like involving outsiders or letting anyone else in. And who could blame him?

Lachlin planted his hands on his hips and said, "Jax, you can be such an idiot. I love you and have done things your way for most of our lives. I need this, and I think I need her. It doesn't mean I love you any less, but I want a *family*, man. I want a woman in our bed permanently."

"And if I don't?" Jax challenged and held his breath.

Anya Summers

Pain filled Lachlin's gaze. "Then I'm sorry. As much as I love you, I need this. It's a yearning I've had for a few years now, but it's only been in the last few months that I have realized I won't be happy without it."

Fear clenched his heart. Anger seethed, stoking his dominant nature. "I will tan your fucking hide for those remarks. Don't threaten me. I will help you but I'm not fucking happy about it."

"Fair enough," Lachlin said. "And you enjoy paddling my ass too much for that to be a hardship for you."

The man knew Jax well. He would discipline Lachlin for this, later, after the little sub had been found. "Let's go find your sub, shall we?"

He shoved his legs into board shorts, grabbed a black tank. and slid his sandals on. He had to rein in his anger but he was having a hard damn time of it. The little violinist was causing him nothing but problems.

"We should split up. In her fragile state, who knows what she is planning on doing?" Lachlin said as he slid his shoes on.

"That's fine. If we don't find her in the next two hours we meet back here, regroup, and then we'll get Jared involved. You need to prepare yourself for the thought that she may be beyond our aid."

Lachlin gave a slight nod of his head as a response. Jax noted the furious set to his jaw as they headed out of their villa. At the trail, they separated, and Jax couldn't help but feel he was losing him. And he had no idea how to stop it. As much as he wanted to blame Amaya, he knew deep down that it wasn't her, it was him.

He headed west out of their villa, starting at the northernmost point of the island, near the employee housing, and then made his way down the coast. The island was a beauty. The sandy beach was pristine and more untouched by man than many of the commercial ones. He found it a bit ironic that Jared would select another locale so far away from civilization. Had he not realized how similar it was to the Scottish manor? As Jax approached the desolate southern tip of the beach, he smelled smoke on the breeze. He scanned the horizon and searched until he located the origin as it billowed up in a solid plume.

Instinctively, he knew it was Amaya. What had she set on fire?

His chest clenched as he picked up his pace, sprinting the remaining distance. It would devastate Lachlin if something happened to her. As much as he didn't want or like her intrusion into their lives, he knew that in order to keep his life the way he wanted it, with Lachlin, he needed to bend a bit on his stance.

Jax found her sitting before a small bonfire she'd created on the beach. She'd even surrounded it with a small stone circle to keep it contained. She looked so damn small and hopeless, he couldn't help but feel for her. He approached the blaze and spied the charring violin case. The violin inside was completely ablaze. That thing was a fifteen-thousand-dollar instrument. He knew that because he'd asked her in Scotland. He tried to imagine what it would take to make him do that to his bass guitar, and felt sucker-punched in the gut.

Oh the poor baby, she was hurting worse than even Lachlin had imagined. Jax's every dominant instinct urged him to protect her. He didn't want to feel that way toward her, but he couldn't stop it.

Tears rained down her face as she gazed hypnotically into the fire. She hadn't even heard him approach.

"What did you do here, pet, hmm?" He used his sexy, I'm-a-rock-star voice, the one that made all his female fans swoon.

Amaya didn't even blink as she turned her distraught, tear-stained face toward him. The sorrow in her eyes was almost tangible.

Christ, he had to be careful here, for both their sakes. He cupped her chin, wiping her tears away, and murmured, "Come on, pet, tell Jax what hurts and I will make it all go away."

"It doesn't matter. None of it." She shrugged but still had a thousand-yard stare behind the sorrow.

That did it. Drastic measures were needed here. It may not be the route Lachlin would use to proceed, but Jax needed to do something. He worried about moving her back to the villa. At her listless response, he hefted her into his arms. She didn't fight him or struggle. And that did worry him. She was more of a fighter than this. Hell, she had given them a run for their money in Scotland. He carried her into the surf and dropped her into the crystal blue water. She came back up for air, sputtering, and screeched.

"Get away from me!" She glared at him in disbelief.

Good. He wanted that spark, wanted to tap into that and make her fight, make her care.

He put on his 'I'm a badass Dom and will not budge until you submit to me, little sub' face and said, "No. You agreed to be our sub, and while I personally think you are far more trouble than you're worth and would rather leave you be, Lachlin needs you. So, for his sake, you are going to pull yourself together and get your ass back to our villa."

"Fuck off," she spat, shoving the cascading wave of her midnight hair from her face.

His anger seethed and in a low voice, he warned, "Careful, Amaya, you are treading on dangerous ground here." He had no compunction about turning her over his knee and giving her the spanking she so richly deserved. Lachlin didn't

73

think that was the way to break through, but look where his gentle approach had gotten them.

Amaya became incensed by his words and pushed at his chest. "Who made you the boss of me? You don't care that I've lost everything. All you care about is your dick. So forgive me," she shoved against his chest again, "if I couldn't give a flying fuck what you want."

The tide slammed into them. The water made her nipples pebble into hard points beneath her tank top. Then she shoved him again. She was spoiling for a fight, but it was time this little sub learned her place. That was enough of this bullshit. Jax hoisted her over his shoulders and she went crazy. He had planned on bodily carrying her back to the villa, but when her foot connected with his solar plexus, he fell to his knees and she scrambled off him, tripping in the process, and landing on her back.

He wasn't really certain how it happened, but one minute they were both pissed off, out of breath and panting, glaring daggers at one another. Then, in the next, he bent forward and wedged himself between her spread thighs. He kissed her with all the fury and fear that had been eating away at his calm. He commanded a response from her and was not disappointed. She returned his kiss with a hunger of her own. There seemed to be a fury inside her as she shoved at his clothing and he was only too happy to oblige. He wanted to pound away his fury, preferably in the taut clasp of her pussy.

Amaya had one of the most kissable mouths, with her top-heavy upper lip. Jax could suck on them for hours. But he didn't seduce. The time for seduction was past for the two of them. Instead, he invaded, her mewling moans against his mouth driving him wild. He ripped her shirt down the center, exposing the small, pert mounds of her breasts. The tan flesh beckoned his mouth and the dark-tipped areolas begged to be sucked on. He latched his lips around one and slurped the hard bud into his mouth. Her back bowed beneath him as she tried to feed him more of her tit.

She was this firecracker of explosive passion and he wanted to master her, make her understand that he controlled her climax.

She still had far too much clothing on as her fingers slid into his hair. Christ, he wanted to fuck her until her legs fell off. He bit down on her nipple, hard. He wasn't being gentle but judging by her bucking hips against his groin, he surmised she liked the pain. It drove his own passion as he peppered her breast with bites until the protruding nipple was red and swollen. Then he did the same with its twin, and all the while she writhed beneath him. He ground his pelvis against hers as the tide swept in around them on the sand.

He needed to feel the sweet clasp of her cunt around his dick. He ripped her pants down the center until she was bare, her pussy lips spread, inviting him into her warm heat. Then he hefted her up, wrapping her arms around his neck. She instinctively wrapped her legs around his waist. He walked with her until they stood in the ocean, the tide billowing around them, and then he undid his shorts, allowing his erection to spring free.

Amaya's eyes were closed as he fit his cock at her entrance.

"Look at me," he commanded. He waited until she followed his command. "Keep your eyes on me, pet, I want you to know who is fucking you, understood?"

"Yes, Sir." She whimpered as he rubbed the crown through her folds.

She moaned as he pressed, using the tide to push his body forward until he was buried in her pussy. He hissed at the tight clasp as she contracted around him. And then he withdrew with the tide before slamming back inside her. He used the natural motion of the ocean as he thrust and withdrew until they were both panting heavily.

He kept his rhythm steady when what he wanted to do was fuck her until his legs gave out. Where had this startling need for her come from? He wasn't certain, but he rode it—and her—until he felt the first flutters of her pussy spasming around his cock. Now was the time.

He stilled his movements. When she whimpered, he asked, "Why did you burn your violin?"

She clamped her lips together. He rocked his hips slightly, just enough to cause friction, and she moaned.

"I will give you what you want, pet, but you need to be honest with me. Lachlin and I cannot be proper Doms for you until you tell us."

Instead of moving, he held her still, embedded deep in her pussy, not allowing her to move her hips. Their battle of wills played out for a few moments while Amaya determined he was not going to allow movement of any kind. She growled in the back of her throat. He hid his smile. She was a feisty one. And he was glad to see some of her spirit returning.

When she didn't respond, he withdrew, and she whined as he carried her back to shore where he unceremoniously set her on her feet.

Before he could turn away, she whispered brokenly, "Wait."

"I'm listening."

"It's brought me nothing but misery. I've worked so hard, and for what? To lose my job, to have my family disown me, to be evicted from my home and left with nothing, and all because of that thing." Her chest heaved with fury and he could tell she was nearly sobbing. He wanted to reward her.

77

He yanked her into his arms and kissed her, rewarding her for being good. He knelt down, pulling her with him in the wet sand until she was straddling him. Then he was furrowing his cock inside her clasping heat and having her ride him. He pumped his hips and she thrust against him, her fingers dug into his shoulders and he reveled in the feel of her wrapped around him.

Over and over he penetrated her sheath in fast, nearly brutal strokes, pounding his cock inside her. She wrapped herself around him, canting her hips and meeting him thrust for thrust. Their movements became almost animalistic in nature, like they couldn't get close enough.

He growled in her ear, "Come for me, pet," and then he slammed home.

"Oh god!" Her body vibrated as she came around him and her high-pitched wails drove him onward as his climax started at the base of his spine. His balls filled and his cock swelled. Between one thrust and the next, his cock thudded, spurting cum inside her clasping, quivering heat to mingle with her juices.

He pounded until the last drops of semen were emptied from his cock. And then he held her as she clung to him and he felt a little piece of his heart crack open. Her trust in him made his belly clench.

When he felt her tears against his shoulder, he withdrew his softening member and resituated them so that she was in his lap. He held her through the storm as her emotions battered her. He was her buffer, stroking a hand down her back, reassuring her as much as he could that he wouldn't leave her to slay her dragons alone. Jax knew all too well how hard that could be.

That was where Lachlin found them. Half-naked, covered in cum, drying sand and salt water, with Amaya nestled in Jax's arms like he was her lifeline.

Lachlin was right, they did need her. It worried Jax just how much.

Chapter Six

Lachlin couldn't believe his eyes. Never in a million years would he have guessed that he would find Amaya and Jax together and, from the looks of it, they had screwed each other something fierce, if the state of the tattered remains of Amaya's clothes was anything to go by.

And he knew well the look Jax got on his face after particularly intense sex—he was wearing it now. Lachlin approached them cautiously. Amaya's face was tear-streaked as he knelt beside them.

"Seems you have both been busy without me," Lachlin teased, not wanting to admit that he was a little jealous that Jax had found her first. He should have come to this location before searching the rest of the island.

Amaya lifted her face and arms to Lachlin. They had a connection. It was a natural extension of them. But he hoped, judging by the state of things, that perhaps she and Jax had found their common ground. Hope bubbled in his chest. He gathered her close, feeling the knot of worry that had been present since he had woken to discover her absence, begin to unravel.

"It's time I get you both back to the villa. For your punishment." Jax stood, readjusting his shorts.

Lachlin's belly clenched. He loved it when Jax disciplined him, but he worried whether Amaya was ready. However, he didn't question Jax. After their fight that morning, he wanted to reassure Jax that his love for him was as steadfast as ever. Lachlin had hated giving him an ultimatum the way he had, but sometimes Jax was so hard-headed when it came to change of any kind, Lachlin literally had to drag him kicking and screaming— or hold his feet to the fire. Lachlin knew that where Amaya was concerned, they had to present a united front. She was too fragile to handle any drama with them right now.

Jax doused the flames from the fire. There wasn't much left but the charred remains of her instrument, but they didn't want to leave it unattended. Lachlin helped her stand, her legs wobbling like a newborn foal's. Seeing her lack of clothing, or what remained of the ripped garments, he stripped his shirt off over his head. Then helped her put it on, removing the remnants of her clothes and shoving them in the small sack she had with her. "Come on, love, let's get you home."

She nodded. He threaded his fingers through hers as they walked back to the path where he had parked their cart. Jax climbed in the driver's seat and Lachlin pulled Amaya into his lap. She was an armful, but one he wanted to hold on to and never let go.

Lachlin knew he just had to prove to her that he and Jax were the perfect Doms for her. He also had to make Jax see how perfectly she completed them. He felt it deep within his bones.

At the villa, Lachlin went directly to the shower. Amaya was filthy from head to toe. He knew she needed his help to wash all the sand, cum, and salt water from her body. Without even asking permission, he took control of the situation and stripped her down, placing her on the small bench inside the glass shower enclosure. Then he disrobed, shucking his shorts before he entered the cubicle with her.

Once he had adjusted the water to the right temperature, he took the loofah from her hands, added soap, and washed her limbs. He started with her arms and her chest, enjoying the way her nipples pebbled at his touch, before working his way down over her belly, between her thighs, and her legs. Her complete trust in him warmed his heart as he shampooed and rinsed her hair, adding conditioner to her gorgeous mane. And there was a spark back in her dark gaze that had been absent since they had arrived on the island.

Because he needed to feel her in his arms, both for her sake, and because he craved her, he kissed her just as Jax stepped into the shower. Lachlin broke the kiss and shot him a glance. Jax, of course, was sporting mega wood. Desire raged inside Lachlin and it was Jax's face that made his balls clench in eager anticipation of the wicked delights Jax had cooked up for them.

Jax was never one to leave him hanging and before Lachlin could say boo about anything, he commanded, "Both of you on your knees."

Lachlin helped Amaya down to the tile floor, then he descended so that he was kneeling beside her. This position placed Jax's impressive cock directly in their line of sight. Lachlin couldn't help but lick his lips in anticipation. Jax was a commanding, demanding lover who loved to fuck. There were days he didn't allow Lachlin out of bed except for the necessities. Jax stroked a hand down Amaya's wet hair. "Open up, pet, and suck me."

Amaya needed no further urging; whatever had transpired between her and Jax had cemented a bond between them, and she did as Jax bid. Holding his bulging cock, Jax fed it into her waiting mouth and groaned. Amaya moaned around his shaft as Jax thrust. Lachlin felt pre-cum leak from his own crown as he hungered to feel Jax's dick in his mouth.

"This is part of your punishment, my love," Jax said. "Watch how she takes my cock in her mouth. Christ, you are good at this, pet. I might make this your job and make Lachlin watch us each time." Amaya moaned around Jax's cock and her nipples pebbled. Lachlin gritted his teeth, entranced with watching Jax's length plunge in her mouth.

Anya Summers

Jax stroked his free hand over Lachlin's head and drew his face near his cock. "Suck on my balls, love, while she sucks my cock, then you can trade off in a bit."

Lachlin didn't need to be told twice, tonguing Jax's heavy sack and slurping the heavy orbs into his mouth. He tongued Jax's perineum, wishing it was his puckered ass. At Jax's garbled groan, he smiled, knowing just how the man liked his balls played with.

Then Jax withdrew his swollen shaft from Amaya's mouth. She whined at the loss, not that Lachlin blamed her at all. Lachlin couldn't help himself and kissed her until they were both breathless and panting. Then Jax's cock nudged against Lachlin's mouth and he opened it, accepting his lover. Not wanting to leave her out of their love play, Lachlin's fingers sought and stroked Amaya's pussy. He rubbed his fingers against her clit as she sucked on Jax's balls. Her cream poured over his fingers as he teased her. He wanted to suck on her, taste her cream just like he was swallowing Jax's delicious cock.

While Lachlin fingered Amaya, she grasped the hilt of his shaft, stroking his hard length. When she squeezed around his dick, her fingers putting pressure on his member, he groaned around Jax's cock plunging in his mouth.

Christ, if he wasn't careful, he would spill his seed before he had a chance to fuck either of his lovers. And that's what they both were. He would prove to them both before this session was over that they were better together. He suckled Jax's thick cock like it was a fine delicacy and felt it swell in his mouth. Jax was fucking his mouth with force, which meant his climax was nearing. As much as Lachlin wanted to taste his lover's cum, he wasn't ready for this to session to end just yet.

He released Jax's cock with a popping sound.

"Continue," Jax ordered, fisting his erection. Lachlin gripped Jax's cock and addressed Amaya, whose pupils were dilated with passion as she licked her lips, staring hungrily at Jax's cock.

"Suck his cock with me, love," Lachlin commanded.

Amaya moaned and needed no further urging as she leaned forward, closing her mouth around the crown and drawing Jax's member into her hot little mouth. She bobbed her head a few times before Lachlin stopped her and said, "My turn."

And that's how they sucked Jax's cock until the water ran cold and the shower was finally shut off. They took turns swallowing Jax's shaft, kissing each other in between as they transferred his dick from each other's mouths. They licked him together, teasing the crown.

Jax was completely gone, passion overriding his features. It was Lachlin who was in charge of their session now. As much as he hungered to taste Jax's cum, he knew he had to let Amaya drink him to forge more of a connection. And Jax was near the edge, with his climax imminent. Lachlin knew the signs as Jax's cock juddered and stretched in his mouth. He released him and gave Amaya a torrid kiss as he stroked Jax's cock with his hand.

"Finish him off, love. Make our Jax cum in your pretty mouth."

She nodded and mewled in the back of her throat. It was so fucking hot watching her open her mouth, desire all over her face as Lachlin fit Jax's member between her lips. Her eyes closed in pleasure as she bobbed her head. Jax unleashed his control, thrusting into her mouth with bruising vigor. It was so hot that Lachlin felt his own cock weep as Jax strained, pummeling Amaya's mouth as he spurted inside her, roaring as he came. Jax finally withdrew his softening member and some of his cum dribbled down Amaya's chin. Lachlin leaned over and licked it up, then took her mouth in a mind-melding kiss. It was a heady experience tasting Jax on Amaya's lips; one he wanted to repeat over and over again.

Then Lachlin broke the kiss and stood, helping Amaya to her feet. He knew they needed to spank her ass for the stunt she had pulled that morning, but right now he needed to be inside her. His cock strained, begging for the sweet clasp of her pussy. Lachlin backed her against the shower wall. She seemed to know exactly what he wanted and opened her arms to him. Using the wall for support, he lifted her up until her legs were firmly wrapped about his waist. He thrummed his fingers against her clit and she moaned into his mouth. Without preamble, he fit his cock at her entrance and thrust into her grasping, greedy channel until he tapped the entrance to her womb.

Lachlin moaned into her mouth as she clasped at his dick. She felt so fucking amazing. He loved her pussy; the way it expanded to accommodate his longer length. Christ, he planned to fuck her until his eyes rolled back in his head. Not wasting any time on formalities, he established a rhythm, using the wall for support and rolling his hips in a thundering pace. Amaya's moans filled the shower, her body wrapped around his. She undulated her hips, meeting his torrid thrusts. And then Jax was at his side, his hand on Lachlin's lower back. Jax leaned in and took Amaya's mouth with his and Lachlin shuttled his cock, ramming her pussy in brutal strokes, watching his lovers kiss each other like their lives depended upon it. Fuck, Lachlin loved having the connection between the three of them. Then Jax's hand slid between Lachlin and Amaya until he was fingering the place where Lachlin and Amaya were most intimately connected.

It felt amazing and made Lachlin pump his hips harder. He wondered what it would feel like if they both penetrated her pussy. Feeling Jax's cock sliding against his while Amaya's pussy grasped at their cocks. Christ, the fantasy almost sent him over the edge. Jax's fingers stroked over her pussy lips, driving Amaya wild, and Lachlin felt his own need increase.

"Fuck her with me, Jax," Lachlin asked on a growl. He needed to do it, craved it with a desire bordering on obsessive. He wanted to feel Jax's cock sliding through her tissues as they fucked her.

Jax swiveled his head, his face dark with desire, and forcefully kissed Lachlin. It was a hard meshing of tongue and teeth that electrified his balls and shot pleasure up his shaft as he pumped into Amaya. Jax grabbed the ever-present tube of lubricant they kept in the shower and slathered his dick with it. Then Jax helped them take a few steps back with his precious cargo, so that Jax was able to slide in behind Amaya. It put Jax up against the shower wall with Amaya between them. Lachlin pressed forward, slowing his pounding hips, with Amaya protesting. He felt Jax begin to work his shaft into her rosette and waited until Jax had penetrated her fully. Amaya was mumbling and moaning, ecstatic in her pleasure as they moved in tandem inside her.

Lachlin thrust and Jax withdrew, and their cocks sliding against each other was the most delicious torture. One of these days, soon, they would take her ass together and her pussy together. Until then, Lachlin reveled in the feel of the taut clamp of Amaya's pussy on his dick as he pummeled her while feeling Jax's cock slide in and out against his shaft.

Their mouths were close as they circled her, holding each other as they fucked her. Amaya's wails as her body quaked between them was enough for Lachlin to let go and he unleashed his control, letting his desire take over. Jax did the same.

The shower filled with their musk as they hammered their cocks inside her. He and Jax grunted at the force of their fucking. And Amaya was beautiful as she took their ramming thrusts, lost in her pleasure, her mouth open on a continual moan, her fingers digging into Lachlin's back where she held on.

"Oh, god," Amaya screamed, her eyes glazed as she moaned. Her body clenched around his cock and he blew his load inside her.

"Ahhh, I'm coming!" Lachlin exploded, filling her grasping channel with his cream. Jax roared as he came and Lachlin felt Amaya's body clench and flutter around his member as another wave of her climax hit.

They stood there, propped against the wall. Amaya laid her head against Lachlin's shoulder as she clung to him. He looked at Jax and knew that he was feeling the same thing. You didn't spend close to two decades with someone and not know them inside out. The three of them shared a tender kiss before the men helped Amaya off Lachlin. Her knees nearly buckled and it was Jax who caught her and carried her into their bedroom, where they all collapsed with exhaustion.

Chapter Seven

Amaya stretched, feeling more replete than she had in an age. She shifted, expecting to find her men. When had they become *her* men?

All she found was empty space. Her stomach rumbled, surprising her. She couldn't remember the last time she had had an appetite. She slid from the bed; the hardwood floor cool beneath her feet. She glanced around the open floor plan and was disappointed that both men seemed to be absent.

After a quick trip to the bathroom, she slid one of Lachlin's tee-shirts on and headed into the kitchen to forage for something to eat. That was when a delicious aroma of grilling meat hit her nostrils and made her mouth water. Following her nose, she opened the sliding glass door that led onto a wooden deck. Jax was standing in board shorts and wielding barbeque tongs as he flipped some heavenly smelling meat. Lachlin was sitting, also wearing shorts, on a patio chair with a beer in his hand.

"Sleeping beauty is awake, I see." Lachlin held out his free hand to her.

Amaya inhaled a deep breath, then closed the distance between them and placed her hand in his. Lachlin drew her onto his lap. His fingers teased the hemline of his shirt on her thighs.

"Looks good on you." He set his beer down on the patio table and cupped her chin.

Amaya's breath caught in her throat as he kissed her. Lachlin kissed her like it was a lazy Sunday morning and they were lying abed with the paper. It was comfort and a hello, and Amaya felt her heart tremble as she returned his embrace. A slow burn ignited in her belly. As much as she was worried about the permanence of this arrangement, she couldn't deny how right it felt being with them.

Then her stomach growled. Lachlin broke their kiss with a chuckle. "Someone sure is hungry."

"Yeah, I am. Starving actually."

"We thought you might be. So we figured steaks were in order. They'll be ready in a minute," Jax said, looking downright sexy as he wielded the tongs.

"Has anyone ever told you that you're quite a beautiful man, Jax? I can see why the groupies go crazy," Amaya said.

He shot her a satisfied male grin. "That's what I live for, pet. The adulation of my adoring fans."

"Don't give him a bigger head than the one he already has, love. The last thing we need is Jax on an ego trip," Lachlin said.

"Can I help it if our sub thinks I'm hot?" Jax gave him a droll look.

"Well, you both are—in different ways, of course." She didn't want Lachlin to think he wasn't attractive. He was, but in a different way. Jax looked like the devil-may-care bad boy you always wanted to try for a night, whereas Lachlin was handsome in a timeless way with his square jaw and steadfast gaze. He made her weak-kneed every time he directed that intense blue gaze of his her way.

Lachlin caressed her bare legs, continuing to tease the hem of her shirt. "I'm glad you find us both appealing to your senses, but don't think this is going to get you out of the punishment you have coming."

"Punishment? Why am I being punished?" She tensed in his arms, trying to recall what she had done to disobey them.

"Do you really think that your little excursion this morning would not warrant discipline? You left without our permission," Lachlin said.

"And you rather epically torched your violin," Jax added.

"I know, but I—"

Lachlin's hands squeezed her thighs gently. "Stop trying to top from the bottom, love. It won't get you anywhere with us. While you are here with us, as our sub, we expect you to have open communication and dialogue with us. We explained that we would help you with what you are going through."

93

She knew that, deep down, she did. "Yes, but—"

"No 'buts' about it, pet, you're getting your just deserts after we refuel," Jax warned with a wave of the tongs in her direction.

At the stern Dom expressions on their faces, she knew they wouldn't budge from their stance. She had been obtuse that morning. Even though she'd had panic and depression swamping her, she should have turned to them and told them what was happening, even if it did mean waking them. She bowed her head in respect and said, "Yes, Sirs."

Jax padded over and lifted her gaze to his. "And if you're a real good girl, I might even let you have my cock again."

She moaned, squirming in Lachlin's lap as she felt his erection form beneath her bottom. Jax chuckled and went back to the grill. Lachlin nipped her bottom lip. "Jax told me about your family disowning you."

She nodded and tears sprang to her eyes. "Yes, they did."

"Tell me what happened," Lachlin said, with comfort and understanding in his eyes.

She shook her head. She didn't want to discuss it and break the spell of contentment she was currently feeling. She wanted to go back to being surrounded by them and feeling loved, not into the pit of despair.

"Don't make me pull it out of you, love. I will if I must, but I would rather you were forthright with us."

She burrowed her face in his chest, not wanting to face it as waves of desolation crashed over her as she thought about it. The image of her father, standing at the door to their house; the way he had looked at her as he had said those things. There had been no love in his gaze, just derision that he was stuck with a daughter who had dishonored him.

Lachlin drew her gaze up to his, and what she saw in his eyes calmed her. He was steadfast and stalwart, more than capable of withstanding the horrible nature of her demise.

She cleared her throat and said, "After I lost my job, I headed home to my parents' house in Kyoto, Japan. There were reporters outside my flat in London while I was being evicted, and I didn't want to be anywhere where the press might follow me. Once I had all my things moved into a storage unit, I went home, thinking it would be safe, where I could figure out what to do about my career. But Edward hated me with a vengeance I didn't understand until I made it home. I'm not sure how he got the address, but he sent copies of the picture to my parents' house as well."

She would never forget the tears in her mother's eyes, nor the disappointment emanating from her father. There were hurts which you never fully healed from, no matter how hard you tried. They were her personal demons that she could perhaps rise above—given time—but with the knowledge that they were always under the surface, waiting and willing to drag her under.

"And what happened when you arrived home?" Lachlin asked gently, guiding her with his calm, soothing baritone.

She could feel the resonance of it in her chest. She took a deep, steadying breath for courage before continuing. "My mother wouldn't speak to me. She just looked at me with this wounded expression and tears in her eyes. I will never forget it. And my father…" Her breath hitched and she felt her heart seize.

"What did he do sweetheart?" Lachlin stroked a hand over her back, attempting to calm her rising panic.

Her heart fluttered in her breast. "He said that I had dishonored the family name, that I was no daughter of his, and cast me out. He told me never to return and threw me away like I was yesterday's garbage," she said, and buried her face in his chest as she expelled a deep sob.

Lachlin's strong arms closed around her. Then she sensed Jax come up behind her. They were constantly surrounding her with their fortitude and acting as her buffer against the world. She feared becoming dependent upon it, because it felt so wonderful having their comfort, feeling their arms around her. She'd never felt so protected in her life.

"We've got you, pet. Lean on us and take some of our strength," Jax murmured into her ear. His hands slid around to her belly.

"Just because your father couldn't see your worth and value doesn't mean others don't," Lachlin said, attempting to help.

"I'm not worth anything," Amaya mumbled through her tears. If her family didn't want to keep her, who would?

"Love, look at me," Lachlin commanded gently, albeit with an edge of steel behind his voice.

It took her a few moments and a few stabilizing breaths to comply with his request as she attempted to pull herself together. She gazed into his face. The wealth of emotion in his eyes made her heart quake.

"You are worth everything. Do you understand?" Lachlin caressed her cheek with his thumb, wiping away her tears.

"And after I paddle your ass for this morning's shenanigans, pet, I will prove it to you," Jax promised with a deep growl as he teased her boobs, tracing his fingers around her nipples.

She laughed through her tears. These two really weren't going to let up until she surrendered everything to them. And she wanted to let go and sink into them with everything that she was.

"Give it time. And we will be here to help you through the worst of the storm," Lachlin said, reassuring her, never taking his gaze off her.

She finally nodded. For them, for what they were trying to do for her, she would try.

Jax kissed her on the temple as he rose. "The steaks are ready. Let's get you fed and then we can begin."

Lachlin carried her inside and set her on one of the chairs at the dining table. Jax followed them inside with a platter of sizzling steaks he placed on the table. They had already put out plates and silverware. Lachlin pulled a few beers out of the fridge and then a salad.

Amaya's eyes closed in pleasure at the first bite of steak. "It's really good," she said after taking a sip of her beer. If she was going to stay there they would have to get some red wine.

"Glad you like it, pet."

"So are you guys off for a while? What's next after the island?" This was something she was extremely curious about.

"Technically, we're off until after the first of the year. It gives us a bit of time to unwind and recover from the grueling nature of touring the world for months on end," Lachlin said.

"While Lachlin may not enjoy our touring as much these days, I tend to thrive on it and will be climbing the proverbial walls by Christmas," Jax added.

98

"And be a pain in the ass in the meantime," Lachlin interjected.

"Hush, love. But we will go back into the studio to work on the next album after the first of January," Jax explained.

"I see. And are you planning another tour?" Amaya asked.

Lachlin said, "Probably in another year or so. We will likely try to schedule the album release with our record company after Bastian and Delilah get hitched."

"And give the newlyweds some solo time before we make Bastian hit the road again."

"That's nice of you guys," Amaya said, thinking she would see them at the wedding and wondering whether it would be awkward after the time they had spent together here on the island. Or would they want to pick up where they left off?

"It's only because we can now, pet. There was a time not too long ago when we wouldn't have had a choice," Jax replied.

"Have you considered what you are going to do?" Lachlin asked Amaya.

"No." And that made her feel like an even bigger failure. "I haven't been able to move past being fired from the symphony orchestra. I didn't have a plan in place after that. Silly and stupid now, in retrospect, but I don't know. I could try for another symphony orchestra, but word travels fast in my world and while people's memories might be short, they don't forgive a blunder like mine."

"We understand. It's one of the reasons why we've been keeping our relationship private and off the radar of the press," Lachlin said.

"Have you considered studio work?" Jax asked Amaya.

"No, not really. It's certainly a thought. But every time I think about playing, I see my father and hear his words. He was the one who put the violin in my hands the first time."

Lachlin's eyes were kind and filled with emotion as he said, "Sweetheart, I have watched you play. The music is inside you. Just because he was the one who started you on your path, doesn't mean you need to punish yourself and never play again. Music is part of who you are, anyone who has watched you play can see that. It's probably why this is hitting you so hard. Your violin is an extension of you, just as the piano and keyboards are for me, or the bass is for Jax."

Lachlin's words hit home. He was right. She had been punishing herself because of her father. He was a stubborn, thick-headed mule, and would hold the grudge against her until the day he died. Did she really want to abandon something she loved because her father wouldn't look past his own nose and accept her for who she was instead of who he wanted her to be?

Now Amaya ached for the loss of her violin. It was a part of her identity. That was why she'd been feeling so lost. Without her violin, a part of her soul was missing. And the anger and rage; those hadn't been directed toward the instrument so much as toward her father. She'd just been in such mental turmoil that she had directed her emotions toward the violin, instead of where it should be.

"And we couldn't have had this little conversation twenty-four hours ago," she said drolly.

Lachlin cocked his head to one side as he contemplated her and said, "You weren't ready yet then. Now you are."

She shrugged. "Yeah, and I just torched a fifteen-thousand-dollar violin. And it's not that money will be an issue, it's just that finding a new one I like will take some time."

"You should make your own studio album," Jax said, taking a swig of his beer.

"You think?" A little thrill shot through her body at the thought. Maybe. Maybe it was a direction she should investigate. It was something; forward momentum after spinning her wheels in misery.

"It's something to consider. Hell, we've thought about adding some extra instruments to our songs. Maybe we could interest you in a collaboration." Jax gave her a wink.

"You would do that for me? Because I'm sleeping with you?" She didn't ever want to be the woman who got where she was on her back.

"No, we would do that because you happen to be one hell of a violinist and we only work with the best. The fact that we could fuck you anytime we wanted to is just a bonus," Lachlin murmured, his voice thick with lust.

"And about that whole fucking thing. Now that we are refueled, it's time for your punishment, pet. No more delays," Jax said.

"Could I just visit the restroom first please, Sir?"

Jax gave her a sardonic glance. "If you must. You have five minutes. Meet us in the dungeon area."

"Yes, Sir." She slid off her stool and made a beeline dash to the bathroom. When she was rinsing her hands off after using the facility, she glanced in the mirror and noticed there was a hint of a smile on her face. Her eyes didn't look dull any more.

That was Jax and Lachlin's doing. They were coming to mean something to her. And it worried her still that now, when she looked to her future, she didn't want one if they weren't in it.

Her core muscles quivered as she walked back into the bedroom and found them waiting by the horse. Her thighs clenched as she walked over to them. She was ready to submit to them fully.

Would they want her for more than just a temporary fling?

Amaya craved permanence in her life; a constant that provided safety and security. And they were both so gorgeous, they took her breath away. They had both stripped while she'd been in the bathroom and stood there, confident in who they were, each sporting an erection that made cream drip from her pussy onto her thighs as she walked.

"As much as I love seeing you in my clothes, love, off with the shirt," Lachlin ordered.

She did as he asked, pulling the black tee up over her head, then folding it and placing it on a bench at the foot of the bed.

Jax held out a hand, which she took without question. Then he led her over to the horse. She let them lift her and position her body until she was straddling the padded black leather on her hands and elbows as they fastened her to the horse. It put her butt in prime position for whatever they had planned.

Lachlin double checked all her restraints before giving her a swift kiss on the forehead. "Remember your safeword is red, love."

Jax ran a flogger over her ass and she shivered in anticipation. "We are going to take turns disciplining you, pet. You offended us both in different ways and this is your atonement. One, you are not to speak unless we permit it—unless you need to use your safeword, where we will stop and

103

re-adjust. Two, and this is the most important rule, you will not come until we allow it. Understood?"

"Yes, Sirs," she breathed on a sigh.

Pain lanced across her exposed buttocks at the first snap of leather against her rear. She gritted her teeth as discomfort burned up her spine. At the second strike, fire ignited in her veins and she tried hard not to cry out. At the third strike, she moaned. She might not be a pain slut, but she adored a good discipline session, usually because it made her so hot that she came multiple times afterward.

Then Lachlin's cock, the beautifully formed crest with a glistening drop of pre-cum, pressed against her lips. "Open up for me, love. My dick should keep your mouth busy and quiet while Jax blisters your ass."

Her mouth opened on his command and she groaned as he thrust his long length down her throat. She flicked her tongue over the head as he pumped his hips. And, through it all, Jax flogged her ass, the strips of leather cracking against her skin and filling the space. She took every blow and reveled in the feel of it. It was as though lava was pouring from her burning ass all the way to her pussy, igniting a maelstrom of desire. Her nipples pebbled painfully against the leather, aching for one of the men to suck them.

Then they switched positions. Lachlin withdrew his erection, leaving her mouth feeling empty and bereft at the loss. But then the bulbous thick crest of Jax's cock pressed against her lips and she opened her mouth once more. Lachlin teased her labia lips with the flogger and she heard him growl, "Christ, you're drenched."

She yelped around Jax's thick member as he fucked her mouth. Lachlin licked her slit and sucked on her cream. Then the biting sting of the flogger whipped against her flesh and dew trickled down her thighs. Lachlin struck her clit with the flogger and it took every ounce of strength inside her not to come.

Lachlin knew just how to strike for maximum impact until she was a writhing, mindless being in need of a good fucking. She would have said so but Jax was currently pumping his cock in her mouth. She loved every minute of it.

"Switch," Lachlin growled, passing the flogger to Jax.

She mewled when Jax withdrew his shaft, but then Lachlin was there, thrusting his length into her mouth. Amaya couldn't squirm away as her butt erupted in flames from the flogging. Over and over, the leather spanked her ass. Her pussy throbbed. She moaned around Lachlin's shaft.

Then Lachlin and Jax both withdrew and she whined. They undid her restraints and before she started to whimper, Jax said, "Not to worry, pet. We are just repositioning you better so we can both fuck you now."

They laid her on her back on the horse, adjusting her legs until they were bent to the point where her heels almost touched the backs of her thighs. They fit a leather strap around each of her thighs and calves to keep them in place, and her ankles were cuffed to the horse. A strap was attached across her lower abdomen and then another one was positioned directly below her breasts. Lachlin affixed cuffs to her wrists, then pulled them above her head, attaching them to the opposite end of the horse. Amaya was completely immobile and at their mercy.

Her stomach was tied in knots in anticipation of the delicious torture as her butt burned against the leather.

Jax double checked her restraints and Lachlin kissed her from where he was standing on the left side of the horse. It was a hungry mingling, meant to remove any barriers she still had in place. She felt them drift away, giving herself over to his kiss. Then Lachlin released her lips and she whined in the back of her throat, wanting more. She always wanted more from him. Jax moved into position on the other side of her and claimed her lips in a fiery possession. The two of them were always a buffer against the world. Jax and Lachlin took turns kissing her. Nothing more than that. She kissed them back. Amaya felt like she was on fire, going up in flames at their commanding domination. At this point, the rest of the world had fallen away and all she could see and feel was them.

And then, as they made to switch, with Lachlin releasing her lips and Jax coming in to pick up where Lachlin had left off, Jax and Lachlin kissed each other. They teased her, just out of her reach. It was a hungry, urgent kiss. It fueled her desire, making her blood pump and her pussy throb. She loved it when they loved one another and that they shared that passion with her. She only wished she could touch them. She moaned when their kiss turned downright feral.

Lachlin and Jax broke apart and the hunger in their gazes nearly sent her off the cliff. Then they turned that passion toward her. The three of them kissed each other, together, their tongues tangling between them.

Lachlin broke away first, and laid a series of open-mouthed kisses along Amaya's jawline, down her throat. Jax followed suit, caressing the opposite side, tracing his tongue over her skin until each man was hovering over a breast. She watched Lachlin's blond head and Jax's dark one descend and envelope each nipple.

"Oh, god," she gasped.

Jax bit down on her nipple as he suckled her in a fast series of bites that sent pleasure arcing directly from her tit to her clit. Lachlin lashed her nipple with his tongue, making the bud swell with his ministrations. Their hands stroked possessively down over her abdomen.

She moaned as their fingers ran through her labia folds. Lachlin ran teasing circles around her clitoris, never touching the bud but making it swell and engorge. Then Jax stole her ability to think as he pressed two fingers inside her, thrusting deep past her swollen lips.

She whimpered, mewling continuously as the waves of her desire rose to earth-shattering new heights.

"Please, Sirs. Please let me come," she begged, thrashing her head from side to side, unable to thrust into the finger fucking from Jax or make Lachlin rub her clit any faster. She wailed and her body strained, ready to reach that shining peak.

"What do you think, Jax, should we let our girl come?"

Jax released her breast with a popping sound. "She has been good, taking her punishment without complaint. I guess we can reward her."

"Come for us," Lachlin ordered, and pinched her swollen clit between his thumb and forefinger. Jax thrust his fingers faster in her pussy. And her world exploded.

Fireworks exploded behind her lids as pleasure ricocheted through her system, her pussy clenching on Jax's fingers as she came. "Oh god, oh god."

But they didn't stop there. Oh no, they planned to use this one session to ensure that she knew with every fiber of her being whom she belonged to. They were mastering her body with all the finesse and knowledge of a maestro conducting an orchestra.

They ate her pussy together. Jax went between her thighs, planting his face over her pussy as he lapped her cream and channel. Lachlin bent over her side and came at her pussy from the top, flicking his tongue over her already swollen clit. Their tongues mingled together and stroked each other as they ate her out. And Amaya floated on a planet of pleasure and desire so thick, she never wanted to come up for air.

They pushed her, taking her to the edge again and again, with Jax adding his fingers to her back sheath, penetrating her ass as he plunged his tongue in her cunt.

She'd never experienced anything so erotic and potent before. Her eyes rolled back in her head as they brought her to orgasm twice. Both times, she screamed, trembling as the orgasms thundered through her body.

Jax and Lachlin stood, her cream dripping down their chins, their cocks jutting from their abdomens. Amaya watched as they licked her cream off each other's faces. And then Jax said to Lachlin, "Get me the cock ring dildo, and some lube. I want to fuck both her pussy and ass together."

She whimpered. But Jax continued, "And while I fuck her, I want that cock of yours in my ass."

It was Lachlin's turn to moan as Jax ordered them both about. Lachlin handed him the beaded cock ring with a full size, fully formed dildo attached to it that was just as long as—albeit thinner than—Jax's cock. She stared, unabashed, biting her lower lip as Jax slid the cock ring over his bulging member, with the slender dildo hanging an inch or so beneath his cock. He slathered lube on her rosette, pushing his fingers back inside and coating her ass. Then he withdrew his fingers and smeared lube over the dildo before handing the bottle to Lachlin.

Her pussy quivered in anticipation of feeling his cock inside her.

Jax lined up his member at the entrance to her pussy and fit the head of the dildo aligning it with her puckered ass. With a roll of his pelvis, he thrust, furrowing both shafts inside her. Her tissues expanded with the pleasure pain of his dual penetration. She gasped, her mouth falling open on a moan as he pushed his way inside.

Amaya was surprised that she wasn't propelled off the planet. Once he had fully embedded himself inside her, he stilled. His face hovered above hers as he bent over her. His hands cupped her breasts, rolling her nipples between his fingers.

"You're doing wonderfully, pet. Give us just a moment for Lachlin, and then I plan to fuck you until your legs falls off," he promised, giving her a wink.

She groaned in the back of her throat. Her pussy quaked around his thick cock.

Then Lachlin positioned himself behind Jax. She watched the expression on Jax's face as he was penetrated by Lachlin. Consummate pleasure contorted Jax's features. Lachlin's face was a deep mask of concentration, colored with potent hunger.

Her pussy throbbed around Jax's dick and he smiled. "Almost there, pet, just another—ahhh, Christ, I love it when you shaft me like that," Jax growled as Lachlin thrust.

"Promises, promises," she whined.

Jax barked out a laugh. "Why, I do believe our sub just complained! We should just fuck each other and make you watch, but I'm loving the feel of your hot little cunt on my dick far too much, sweetness. I'll spank you later."

She wanted him, too. Wanted it all from them, and moaned, "Yes, please, Sirs."

"As you wish," Jax murmured.

And then they moved in unison, withdrawing and thrusting almost like synchronized swimmers, although this was synchronized fucking. These two powerful,

111

gorgeous men had invited her to share in their bounty. Amaya was so full she was overflowing as Jax pumped his cock and the dildo inside her. She was mindless, in a sea of pleasure that she never wanted to end.

But as her ardor rose, so did theirs, and they began to thrust faster. Jax hammered her pussy to the point where she saw stars behind her closed lids.

Her body began to unravel and she let go. Jax pummeled her harder. The sounds of their lovemaking, the wet smacking, filled the space. Jax and Lachlin no longer held back. Their moans joined hers as they fucked. And they did indeed fuck. It was no gentle lovemaking, but a furious race to the finish line.

Amaya's control snapped first, seeming to set off a chain reaction in her men.

"Oh god, I'm coming. Oh, oh, ahhh." Tidal waves smashed against her system as her body shook. Her pussy vibrated, clenching, and clasping at Jax's cock. Her ass erupted in a series of spasms, trying to pull the dildo deeper as she came unhinged. As her body went nuclear around Jax's, he strained, his cock jerking as he spurted his cum inside her wet heat. Then Lachlin tensed, shouting his own release.

They both continued thrusting until the final vestiges of their combined orgasms had diminished. Then they stayed that way, fused together as their heart rates slowed, awash in their afterglow haze. Lachlin withdrew first, on unsteady legs, and walked around to the top of the horse where he began to undo her restraints. Then, on a grunt, Jax stood, gliding out of her pussy and ass.

She whimpered as he undid the cuffs on her legs, straightening out her limbs. Once all her restraints had been removed, they helped her off the horse. When her legs buckled from having been in that position for so long, Lachlin scooped her up in his arms and didn't allow her to fall. Her steadfast Dom carried her into the bathroom, with Jax hot on his heels, and started a bath for her. They both climbed in and held her body between them. Jax kissed her, his lips tender as they danced with hers. Then he kissed Lachlin and she watched their hungry duel. Then it was Lachlin's turn to kiss her, and he claimed her lips so sweetly, stroking her cheek, that her heart trembled.

Amaya floated on a cloud as they relaxed in the hot water, and wondered what they would think if she asked them to keep her. Would they want to love her forever instead of just for a little while?

Chapter Eight

Amaya awoke hours later to the strains of an electric keyboard and bass playing. It was a melodic ballad, and it made her think of floating on a boat at sunset. Sitting up in bed, she was enamored of Lachlin's fingers as they flew over the keys in the heartrending melody. Was it any wonder they could play her body with such finesse?

Jax had parked himself on one of the chairs. His black and white Fender bass guitar was resting on his thigh as he strummed the strings, his fingers sliding up and down the neck in a graceful dance.

"Wait, what if you used the key change and added a six, four, five chord progression like this?" Jax demonstrated. Lachlin nodded in time to the beat.

"I like it. Again, from the top. I have a few embellishments I'm going to add to see how they sound."

Amaya rose from the bed, entranced by the music they were making. She grabbed one of the guys' shirts and slid it on as she tiptoed into the living room. She didn't want to disturb their creative process. Blank pages of sheet music lay on the coffee table.

They played through the eight measures again. Then Lachlin added a beat with his keyboard.

When they had finished, grinning at each other, Amaya clapped and their gazes shot to her. The looks in their eyes made her blood heat.

"I liked it. What's it called?" she asked.

"Sleeping beauty, awake at last. Sleep well, pet?" Jax gave her a cocky grin, like he knew he had screwed her brains out and was pleased as punch about it.

"Like a baby. And you?" she said honestly, because she had. Sex with the two of them had been the absolute best medicine. Her body had unwound from its heightened state of anxiety and she'd slept more deeply and peacefully than she had in weeks.

"If I'd realized having you beneath me on a regular basis would make the insomnia go away, I wouldn't have let you leave the manor in Scotland, pet." The intensity of Jax's heated gaze made her stomach tumble and her nipples harden.

Needing to distract herself from the startling, sudden aching need pounding through her body, she turned to her other Dom before she ended up begging them to fuck her. "And you, Lachlin?" she asked.

Lachlin's eyes roamed over her form. She was in what she surmised was his shirt by the slightly woodsy smell. "Never better. I like seeing you in my shirts, love. It makes me want to strip you out of them," he teased.

Her cheeks heated and she was sure her blush showed. She cleared her throat. "What are you working on?"

"Jax here had an idea for a song and, well, here we are."

"Like the words, and everything?"

"No," Jax said. "I woke up with this awesome riff running through my mind and had to write it down. Lachlin heard me moving about, strumming the bass, and joined me."

"Don't mind him. When it comes to writing new songs, he's a little mental, that one." Lachlin nodded toward Jax with a grin.

"Could I help?" She had the beat in her mind.

Jax cocked his head to the side, contemplating her for a moment before he said, "Have you ever played bass guitar?"

"Sadly, no. I was never allowed to play anything other than my instrument growing up. My father wouldn't allow it. I'll never forget when I brought a drum kit home."

"Well, step right up and have a seat. Let me show you a few chord progressions and then I can work out Collum's guitar notes." Jax patted the chair beside him.

Amaya spent the morning with them making music. She found herself smiling and laughing outright at the banter between her two men. And they were hers. In her heart, she was claiming them as much as they had claimed her body. She had forgotten just how much fun making music could be when she wasn't on task to perform, to perfect a piece until it was played precisely how the conductor wanted it to be.

She couldn't ever remember having had this much enjoyment while playing. She had relished playing with Ian, Elizabeth, Soloman, Olivia, and Delilah at Declan's wedding. But this right here, with Lachlin and Jax, was different on so many levels. It was pleasurable. They listened when she made suggestions for a different chord progression and changing the time signature.

When else had she ever had anyone respect her insights? Never. Not in twenty plus years of playing the violin. Not her conductor, not her fellow string section in the orchestra—she had just been there to blindly play whatever was put before her. But this: the possibilities, the notes and different chord progressions, the key signatures. She could play without the orchestra. She could create the music she wanted to play. She knew how to write music but she had been too scared and, if she were honest, too busy with the demands of the orchestra to even attempt to break free and write any for herself.

Excitement flooded through her veins at the prospect. She cursed her stupidity for torching her violin. She could play any one, it didn't matter whether it cost a hundred dollars or fifteen thousand. Maybe she had needed to watch it go up in flames, the symbolic nature of it, like she was torching her old life and beginning anew. It wasn't like she was hurting for money. She had made plenty playing with the orchestra, and had invested wisely.

Lachlin was the one to call it quits on their music creation. "Love, I'm sorry, but Jax and I have a Dom meeting at the main hotel in thirty minutes that will likely take up the afternoon. Do you want to come into the resort with us?"

Amaya realized she could use one of the computers there to purchase and order a violin and have it shipped to the island.

"I would like that. They just rolled out the spa and I would love to get a pedicure."

And it would give her a chance to look in the shop for some club wear. She had some with her but she wanted something special that would drive them over the edge.

Jax smacked her ass. "Get ready, pet. And if you're very good, and dressed and ready in under ten minutes, I'll finger you on the drive in." Her knees went weak. She was becoming addicted to their loving. And she didn't know if that was a good thing or not. Neither of them had said whether they wanted more beyond the island.

Amaya dressed knowing that, if the time came, she would beg. It went against her nature. She didn't chase people. She never had—it had always been her philosophy that if you do your thing, the right people, the ones who were supposed to be in your life, would come—and stay.

They were right for her; not one over the other. Both of them.

Jax didn't lie. In the cart on the fifteen-minute ride to the hotel, he finger-fucked her. He brought her to orgasm not once, but twice. And then, in the golf cart parking lot, Lachlin decided he had to have a turn. By the time she walked into the main hotel, she felt like she could do with a nap after three delicious orgasms.

They each gave her a kiss. "It should be over in two hours. Meet us here in the lobby and we'll head back to the villa together."

"Yes, Sirs. Enjoy your meeting." She bowed her head as they left and headed to the elevator. She waited until the elevator doors closed behind them before she sprang into action.

First, she headed into the island gift shop. It had a little bit of everything, from fetish wear, to vibrators, and extra restraints on one side, while the other was more like a convenience store with groceries, toiletries, and there was an entire section with island wear; from bikinis, to beach towels, and coffee mugs, all bearing the resort's logo. She headed into the fetish wear section, where she found a black leather bra and panties duo. The bra circled her smaller breasts and made them look like offerings. The panties were crotchless and were more for looks than functionality, aside from giving two randy Doms easy access. Then she found a black fishnet dress that hugged her every curve and ended at mid-thigh. It teased with glimpses of skin and complimented the bra and panty duo underneath. It was perfect. She bought them and a jeweled diamond butt plug. Jax and Lachlin would lose their minds when they spied her in this get up. Her mind was already turning at how she would surprise them.

Just the thought of what they might do to her when they spied her in this outfit made her pussy throb in anticipation. After her purchases were made, she headed into the computer business center and did a search for music stores on Nassau. It seemed as though luck was on her side for a change. Not only did she locate a shop on Nassau, but when she called them, they had a selection of violins available for purchase—some of which were potentially what she was looking for in a replacement. Amaya took down all the information, feeling like she finally had a life purpose again.

She checked with reception and discovered there was a boat leaving in ten minutes.

"Could I have someone deliver my purchases to villa nine, Yvette? I need to make a quick run to Nassau," she asked. This was so much more important than getting a pedicure. She could do that tomorrow. She needed this, today—needed to prove she had a purpose again.

"Certainly. And I will call Shep to let him know to expect you. If you want, you can grab one of the boxed lunches from the restaurant and take it with you," Yvette said, ever the hostess.

"That would be fantastic. You are a godsend," Amaya replied.

"On Sunday, while the Doms are watching football in the club, the island subs are planning to have a tea party in the spa. You're welcome to join us. There will be some free beauty treatments and there's a rep from a pleasure party store in the States who will be here and is bringing some new toys for us to try out."

"That sounds like fun. I will make sure Jax and Lachlin know about it."

"Good. It will be nice to get the chance to talk with someone else who has her hands full with more than one Dom." Yvette winked.

"You too, huh?" Amaya cocked her head and studied the pretty brunette.

"Oh yeah, and I could never go back to just one," Yvette murmured.

Amaya understood the sentiment. "I look forward to it."

"Me too. Have fun in Nassau." Yvette picked up the phone and rang Shep to inform him Amaya was headed to him for transport to the island.

Amaya walked over to Master's Pleasure and picked up a boxed lunch and bottle of water, then headed to the docks. It shouldn't take her too long to get to the island, pick out a new violin, and then head back. The guys would just assume she was still in the spa and wait for her. This was something she needed. And she needed it with a fierce vengeance. Even though she was submissive through and through, she had always been self-sufficient. That had been part of her concern: that she would be forced to rely upon other people, depend upon them for her most basic needs.

She boarded Shep's boat and took a seat down below. That way she could eat and plan her next moves. She had a notebook which she wrote in while she munched on a spinach salad with roasted sweet potatoes, caramelized onions, figs, goat's cheese, and balsamic dressing. It was fabulous; one of the best salads she'd had in a while, and she wanted to lick the box clean.

Although, part of that could be the return of her appetite. It had been absent the previous month, but in the last forty-eight hours, it had returned with a vengeance. She finished the entire salad and wished she had grabbed a muffin or two. She would have to get something in Nassau to tide her over. It didn't hurt that she was burning so many calories with all the sex she had been having of late. At the rate they were going, she'd need to start eating every two to three hours to keep her stamina up.

Within an hour, the boat docked in Nassau. Amaya caught a taxi cab to the music store and it was no more than a ten-minute drive. Diadem Music Centre was an eclectic store brimming with stock. Amaya was flabbergasted by the number of violins they stocked. She had a vast selection to choose from. When the owner realized she could play and knew her instrument well, he insisted on pulling out a few for her to play. She located a vintage 1790 British violin in almost mint condition. Its sound wasn't as crisp as her last violin but it would do for now.

She purchased the violin and finally glanced at the time. Cripes! She'd lost herself in the enjoyment of selecting a new instrument and had been in the store for two hours. She thanked the owner and caught a cab back to the docks.

Shep growled as she ran up the boarding plank. "You're late. I was about to send a search party for you."

"I'm so sorry, Sir. I got held up," Amaya apologized and wondered what she would say to Jax and Lachlin. Shep got them underway before she was even seated on the boat deck.

"What was so important?" Shep asked as he sailed them out of the harbor.

"I needed a new violin. My other one got damaged and I need to play." She held the case and all its contents to her chest.

"Well, there's a squall blowing in and I want my boat docked in Pleasure Island before it hits. Get yourself seated below decks, and buckle up. It's going to be a bit bumpy."

"Yes, Sir." She hurried below and did as he bade. She was already going to be in deep shit with her Doms, she didn't need a third one angry with her. Amaya pulled out her phone to call them and realized she didn't have their numbers.

The closer the boat sailed to the island, the more dread settled in her stomach. The euphoria she'd experienced earlier was replaced by mind-numbing fear. Would they walk away from her? Say she was too big of a hassle and not want her anymore? Her family had known her for her entire life and had no problem cutting her out of their lives when she didn't behave in the way they deemed acceptable. So why should a pair of Doms she'd spent less than a week with want to keep a disobedient sub around?

Amaya had to remind herself to keep breathing. She just had to remember to breathe. Jax and Lachlin were nothing like her family. They were warm and loving, accepting her for who she was. They would understand. She repeated the litany as her heart pounded in her chest.

She replayed that mantra in her mind, doing everything in her power not to descend into a panic attack. Shep drove the boat as though the furies of hell were after them, getting the boat to the docks at Pleasure Island in under an hour.

When she disembarked, she spied Jax and Lachlin, standing ramrod straight on the dock. Fury emanated off them in waves. Her insides quaked. What would they do? The panic she'd fought so hard to contain and defeat gripped her in a chokehold. She approached them on shaky legs.

"Sirs, I—"

"Get in the cart, Amaya," Lachlin bit out. His blue eyes had turned almost black in their fury.

Jax didn't even speak to her, he just put a hand on her lower back and forced her feet forward. She clutched her new violin like it was a lifeline. Once she explained, everything would be fine. They may be mad but they would discipline her and they would move on from this.

In the cart, she put her sunglasses on to hide the tears as they fell. Jax drove and both men remained silent.

Back at the resort, they ushered her into the elevator and then the villa. On pins and needles, wondering how bad the punishment would be, she held the violin case to her chest and bowed her head, praying to whoever would listen that this would work out.

Lachlin took a seat on the couch. He patted his lap. "Put what I expect is a new violin down and lay yourself over my knees. You will be punished and made to understand that what you did today can never happen again."

"I'm sorry, Sir, I just needed—"

125

"Silence," Lachlin snapped rather harshly, cutting off the excuses she had on her tongue. Harsh enough that she was taken aback by his tone. He was well and thoroughly pissed. "I did not give you permission to speak. I expect your ass over my knees in ten seconds or less. Don't make me tell you again."

She did as he bade, putting her violin on one of the chairs. Jax was in the kitchen, and she wondered what he had planned for her. But she couldn't focus on him. She had to concentrate on Lachlin, putting one foot in front of the other as she walked to him and the discipline he planned to mete out. Her belly knotted and she called herself a fool for the hundredth time in the space of a minute. Somehow, she always managed to muck things up.

Gingerly, she positioned herself so her rump was exactly where Lachlin had asked her to place it. She didn't want to antagonize him any further. Before she could take another breath, he yanked her shorts and panties down to her knees in one move. She heard the fabric of the shorts rip but said nothing. She deserved this, and maybe, if she took the punishment without giving them a problem, they wouldn't cast her aside. He laid his forearm across her lower back to hold her steady. Then his free hand thwacked against her bare bottom and stole the breath from her lungs at the sharp, stinging pain that brought tears to her eyes.

"These," he laid another three fast, hard swats on her butt, "are so that you understand that what you did today was unacceptable."

"Yes, Sir," she whimpered. He tanned her hide with another five blistering swats and her rear burned like the fires of hell.

"Those were for the worry and concern you caused me when you were nowhere to be found on the island. As your Doms, it is our job to protect you, and it is your job to inform us where you plan to go."

He laid a profusion of rough spanks on her rump that brought tears to her eyes. He was blistering her rear. This wasn't with an intention to turn her on but to make it hard for her to even sit down. She could tell he wanted her to remember this.

"My turn," Jax said, pulling her across his lap. It put her face above Lachlin's thighs. She turned her head to the side and laid it down, needing to feel him, that he wasn't withdrawing from her, that she wouldn't lose him over this.

Then it was Jax's hand connecting with stinging slaps against her ass cheeks. "I was going crazy not knowing where you were. You disrespected both myself and Lachlin. All we have ever wanted was to bring you happiness and satisfaction, and today you proved that it doesn't concern you."

127

Shame flooded her body. He was right, although she hadn't meant it that way and tried to explain, "But I didn't mean to. That wasn't my intent."

"Stop. Trying. To. Top. From. The Bottom. Never before have I had the misfortune to be saddled with a sub who doesn't know the first thing about truly submitting," Jax said, with fury lacing his voice. He gave her three more hard swats. And then he deposited her on Lachlin's lap as though he couldn't get away from her fast enough.

"Lachlin, I know you care for her, and I do, too, but maybe she's not the one for us. I need a breather. I'll be back in a bit." Jax stormed out of the villa, slamming the door to the deck as he exited.

The vibrations from his departure, combined with his words, all but ripped her heart from her chest. Amaya cried, knowing she had lost something before she ever fully had it. Her sobs filled the room as everything fell apart again. Just when she thought she had something she could finally call her own, it was taken from her. She scrambled off Lachlin's lap and went to her suitcase. She started putting her things into the case, including the outfit she had purchased that day, which was still in the bag. She should just return it. She was no good as a sub. She was no good as a daughter.

She was no good, period. And she was leaving.

Chapter Nine

Lachlin's heart squeezed. He knew Amaya was the one for them. Granted, she wasn't the easiest sub in the world, but she was just perfect for them. He would convince Jax of that—he must know it, or he wouldn't be so pissed off at Amaya right now. And, well, the feeling was mutual. Lachlin wanted to tan her hide until it was ruby red. Make her understand the danger of heading off to Nassau without an escort. Especially after what they had discovered at the meeting today; that women were being kidnapped on the islands and being sold into the sex slave trade.

Jared had explained that they needed to be extra vigilant in terms of heading to any of the other islands. He also had his security team patrolling the shore line to make sure there weren't any unexpected visitors to the island's shores.

When he and Jax had left the meeting only to discover she was nowhere to be found, Lachlin had created all sorts of disastrous scenarios that could have played out. It was Jared who had helped them figure out where she was when he questioned the staff.

Lachlin took a deep breath, needing to steady his anger. And then he took another, trying to bring logic and compassion back to his actions before he turned to deal with the little termagant.

Amaya was in the bedroom, hastily shoving items into her suitcase. Her tears fell fast and furious. She trembled and was shaking so violently, still bare from the waist down, that he knew a strong wind would topple her over.

"What the fuck is this, Amaya?" Fear clenched Lachlin's heart. First Jax was behaving badly, now Amaya. She wasn't leaving him. He wouldn't allow it. He loved her too much to let her go. That gave him pause. He hadn't expected to love her, but he did. Deep down, he had hoped it would evolve into the type of connection he had with Jax. But at the present time, he wasn't necessarily happy about it. Christ, what a pickle.

"Look, Lachlin, it's not working with the three of us. You know that, Jax knows that, and I do, too. I appreciate what you have tried to do for me over the last few days. I will never be able to repay your kindness," Amaya said.

Lachlin's inner Dom roared to the surface. "I didn't release you from our bargain and neither did Jax. Stop trying to top from the bottom, Amaya. Until I release you, you are still my sub until further notice. You need to stop running from your problems every time things get difficult."

"But I wasn't—"

He drew her into his arms. Force didn't work, soothing her didn't work, passionate sex didn't work, but he was determined to crack the wall she'd placed around her heart and soul. Instead of tanning her hide again, he kissed her with the single-minded thought that she would know she belonged to him by the time they were finished. He invaded every recess of her mouth, hoping he invaded her heart too, as he stormed her defenses. Lachlin needed to make her trust him, trust that when the going got tough, he wouldn't desert her. Her father's abandonment at her darkest hour had clearly left an indelible mark. Lachlin needed to prove to her that she could make a mistake and he would still be there for her, no matter what. Lachlin was determined to make her blossom. He kissed her until he felt her melt against him. It was only then that he released her lips.

"Get into bed," he ordered, his breathing heavy.

She shook her head. "I don't think—"

"That wasn't a suggestion. Be a good little sub, strip the rest of your clothes off, and lie down in bed. I will join you in a moment." He needed a minute to calm the Dom inside, the one who wanted to turn her back over his knee and spank the living daylights out of her. But that type of force would backfire tenfold; he knew it as surely as he knew he loved her.

"Yes, Sir," she said, her voice hitching around a silent sob.

His heart broke for her. They had to get past her fear of abandonment or they were never going to have a future together. And he did want that, beyond just the next week on the island. He wanted to go the distance with her. He could see it with perfect clarity; his child at her breast. And he wanted it with a fierceness that rattled his core.

Amaya followed his dictate to the letter. When she wasn't gripped by her fear, she was the total sub package. He would get to the bottom of why she had gone to Nassau on her own today, ensure she understood the gravity of the situation, and foster a bond with her that was stronger than her fears. Force didn't seem to work, so instead he would seduce her until he was so emblazoned upon her soul that she would never again try to leave out of fear. Only then could they begin to have the committed relationship each of them craved, including Jax. Lachlin would have to convince him, as well, but he was choosing one battle at a time, and Amaya was the most critical. Jax would come around.

"Now, during this session, you will earn rewards for your honesty. Any dishonesty will be punished." He fastened her wrists and ankles into Velcro restraints. Then he stripped out of his shirt but kept his shorts on. He would only sink his cock into her pussy once he had finished pushing her limits. She was stubborn enough that that would likely take some time. And he didn't want to push his own limits.

He grabbed a few items from the dungeon chest and set them beside her on the bed before

Anya Summers

fitting a black satin blindfold over her eyes. He wanted her completely reliant on him, and by taking away her sense of sight, hoped to make her focus solely on his touch.

"If at any time, it gets too intense, you are allowed to use your safeword: red. Do you understand?"

A shiver went through her body—of fear or anticipation or both, he wasn't sure—and then she responded, "Yes, Sir."

"Good." He could only pray the rest went as smoothly.

Lachlin climbed into bed, situating himself between her spread thighs. He had to bite back a groan at the wetness glistening at her sex. Her body was already attuned to his and Jax's—this was all about invading her heart and soul. He began at her mouth, tracing a delicate line over her lower lip. She gasped. He loved the little sounds she made.

*****

Amaya clenched her hands into fists at the gentle caress. She darted her tongue out, stroking his fingertip. She enjoyed the dark, woodsy flavor of his skin. And then he removed his fingers, planting feather-light kisses on her brow, her cheeks, the corners of her mouth. She wanted his lips on her mouth, dammit. She wanted his kiss.

"Why did you go in to Nassau today?" he asked.

134

"Because I wanted a new violin," she said. That was an easy question.

At her reply, he gave her a soul stealing kiss that left her begging for more. She whimpered when he withdrew.

"And why couldn't it wait until Jax or I could go with you?" he asked, his fingers tracing the outline of her neck.

Amaya didn't want to answer this question, because it made her seem so pathetic. When she tried to turn her face away in shame, he held her firm. She couldn't see his expression but she could imagine the rigid set to his jaw.

"Amaya, answer me, please. Don't make me discipline you."

She clamped her lips shut. Whatever discipline he wanted to do would be preferable to looking like an idiot.

"Fine. Have it your way," he said. Lachlin's lips closed around her breast. He was aggressive as he sucked on her nipple, making the peak engorge and swell until it was almost painful. Lightning arced from her breast to her pussy, creating a vortex of need in her belly. Her blood heated, scorching her insides at his touch. Then he fastened a clamp around her swollen nipple and she hissed at the pleasure pain. Sparks flooded her veins, and her pussy throbbed. He performed a similar action with its twin, working the nub until it was a hard point and then affixing a clamp around it. Her breasts ached, throbbing in time with her clit. Once both clamps were in place, he tugged on them at the same time using a chain connecting the two. Liquid fire erupted in her veins, making a beeline for her clit.

If this was his idea of punishment, she would take it, she thought. This really wasn't so bad. He would screw her brains out and forget about his questions. Then they could go back to being happy and blissful.

"Are you ready to tell me? Why did you leave without telling us? As your Doms, even temporarily, it didn't cross your mind that it was something we should know? That your actions were disrespectful and gave us the impression you don't care a smidgen about us or our feelings? That perhaps you don't want us to be your Doms?"

Shame intertwined with fear and suffused her being. She couldn't lose them; not yet, they had become her bastions against the dark tides. If they let her go, she would drown again, and Amaya didn't know if she would come back from it a second time. "I never intended to hurt you or Jax, you've both been so understanding. I didn't mean it that way at all."

"Then what did you mean, love?" His hands teased the flesh of her stomach, tracing circles and edging closer to her sex.

"I've never had more than a passing fancy with a Dom before; with my traveling and schedule, there wasn't time for anything permanent. So I just didn't think it would be a big deal because I've always had to do for myself. And I thought I would be back by the time you were finished with your meeting. I didn't expect to get caught up playing again at the music store."

"I see. Let me see if I understand you correctly. You were planning to hide your excursion from us and didn't think it was important that you fill us in on where you were headed?"

"No. I just didn't think it mattered to anyone what I did."

"And why would you think that?" He traced her breasts, teasing the clamped nipples and messaging the mounds of flesh.

Amaya clamped her lips shut again. He was making her open her heart to him. Tell him her deepest and darkest secrets. Where would that leave her once he was through with her? She turned her face away. She knew it was an act of defiance. But in that moment, she just didn't want to go there. It would hurt too much. And she didn't want to give him any ideas on how to be rid of her.

"So that's how it's going to be, huh? Have it your way, but don't say I didn't warn you."

Her belly clenched. What did he plan to do? Thankfully, she didn't have to wait long to find out. His fingers stroked between her labia lips, teasing her folds, and she moaned in the back of her throat. He circled her clitoris, stroking above and below

137

her hood, teasing her with his touch but never hitting that one glorious spot. If he was attempting to drive her crazy, it was working. Then his tongue followed suit, like he was learning every crevice and divot, sliding his tongue under her hood and learning her taste.

She was about to complain when he curled his tongue around her clit and penetrated her sheath with two fingers. The unexpected combination sent whirls of pleasure pounding through her body. Her nipples stabbed toward the ceiling and the clamps became even more painful.

Lachlin thrust his long fingers, swirling his tongue, and sucking on her nub. Her pussy clasped at his fingers as they plunged inside, trying to draw them deeper. She couldn't move her hips and make him finger fuck her faster. She could feel her orgasm so close, yet just out of reach.

"Oh god, please let me come," she begged.

Then he slid a cool metal clamp around her engorged clit. The pleasure pain sparked through her system. And she whimpered.

She could feel him withdraw. "Please, Sir, please let me come."

"Then answer the question. Why didn't you inform us?"

"Because I didn't think it would matter to you. My family tossed me away like I was yesterday's garbage. Why would someone I've known for such a short amount of time care? I'm not someone people keep." Tears she hadn't expected suddenly leaked from her eyes. She was glad for the blindfold, as it caught most of them.

"Well, we do care. And we don't have any plans to discard you."

"Jax does, and you love him. What happens to me when you both decide—or he decides—you're done with me? I'll be tossed away again." She shifted her head to the side. "I'd like to stop now please, Sir."

"We aren't finished, love." And then he tilted her face back up and claimed her lips. It was a drugging, slow kiss suffused with emotion. It felt like he wanted to own her body and soul, and with each stroke of his tongue inside her mouth as he plundered her very depths, she wanted to let him. Amaya returned his kiss, greedily accepting his possession. She wanted to be owned by him, wanted to belong to him, wanted to be loved by him in the worst way.

When he broke the kiss, she whimpered. He tugged at a chain which apparently connected all three clamps. Her body nearly combusted. The hot lava of lust poured through her veins and she moaned.

And then his mouth was at her pussy again, plunging his tongue inside her wet heat. He ate her out like a starving man presented with a buffet. Before Amaya could grab a foothold of control, her body splintered and she came in fractured waves.

139

"Oh, god!" She mewled as her body quaked.

But Lachlin didn't stop, he drove her body up another precipice. And then, with a swipe of his tongue against her swollen clit, he stopped.

"Why was it so important for you to get the violin today?"

She growled and whined together; a noise like an animal caught in a snare.

"Amaya, please, love."

"After this morning, when we were making music together, I felt like I had hope for my future again for the first time in weeks. I'd never considered making music on my own or in a studio with other musicians. I guess it was stupid of me not to, but I've always toed the line and played in orchestras. Then this morning, being included and made to feel like I belonged, I realized I didn't want that to end. And I thought that if I could play with you, you would see my worth and want to keep me."

Her blindfold was removed. Lachlin's face hovered above hers, his blue eyes bright with emotion. "I've always known your worth, love. It's time for you to believe it and see it, too. I'm not going anywhere. Do you understand? For better or worse, you are mine, you belong to me, and I won't be letting you go anytime soon."

He kissed her tenderly then, so sweetly it brought more tears to her eyes. "You really do want me?" She searched his expression as he pulled back.

The mattress depressed beside her and Jax said, "We both do, pet."

Jax kissed her breathless then. She had no idea how much he had heard of her confession, or how long he had been standing there. She was just so happy he was back and that he was with them. She strained to kiss him, but her restraints were limiting her movements.

Then she felt Lachlin's crown at her entrance. She gasped into Jax's mouth as Lachlin plunged his shaft inside her to the hilt while Jax kissed her deeply. He lay beside them as Lachlin thrust inside her sheath like a battering ram. Jax toyed with the nipple clamps, rubbing his fingers over them and driving her mindless with need. She moaned into his mouth as Lachlin pumped his firm length inside her. He was so long, he hit the entrance to her womb.

Desire swamped her system. She didn't want to be without her men ever again. Whatever she needed to do to ensure that they kept her, she would do.

Jax released one of the nipple clamps just as Lachlin slammed inside her, and Amaya came apart at the seams.

"Mmm, oh god!" she cried, her body vibrating from the force of her climax. She whimpered as Lachlin withdrew his still erect cock.

But then Jax took his place and was sliding his thick cock into her sensitive, clasping tissues.

Lachlin turned her head toward him, taking her mouth in a torrid mingling of tongues and lips as Jax thrust inside her, rolling his hips and taking her body for a ride. They were all connected, the three of them. She didn't want Lachlin without Jax, or vice versa. The two men were a package deal, and she reveled in being the sole focus of their world.

Amaya loved them. She wanted them not just for tonight, but for always.

She hissed as Lachlin released the other nipple clamp, and the sudden, sharp pain ricocheted through her and transformed into another orgasm so huge, her pussy clasped at Jax's huge dick and she screamed into Lachlin's mouth.

Jax and Lachlin both withdrew from her body. They undid her restraints and released her clit from the clamp. She keened at the exquisite torture as blood flowed back into her abused nub. Then the men both massaged her tight limbs.

"Love, Jax and I are going to try something here. I need you to follow our orders explicitly, okay? We are going to double penetrate and fuck your gorgeous pussy together."

She nodded. "Yes, Sirs."

She'd never experienced double pussy penetration before. She had witnessed it in a club once, and it was one of the hottest scenes she'd ever had the pleasure of viewing. And now she had the chance to experience it with these two. They always put her pleasure and her needs at the forefront of their actions, and the mere thought of feeling both of them so snugly inside her melted her like a smelting fire. Her pussy quivered in anticipation. Jax propped himself up against the headboard, placing a few pillows behind him. He drew her to him.

"Sit on my cock, facing away from me, pet," Jax murmured, assisting her. Lachlin was there too, guiding her down onto Jax's thick length until she was fully seated. Each one of her legs was bent at the knee and canted over his so Jax could spread both their thighs to give Lachlin space between them. Then Lachlin advanced until he was wedged between their thighs.

"Look at me, love. If at any time, something hurts or doesn't feel right, you need to remember to use your safeword," Lachlin ordered.

"Yes, Sir." She squirmed on Jax's lap and his hands clamped on her hips to hold her steady.

"Don't move until we tell you to, pet. We don't want to accidentally hurt you."

"Yes, Sir." She bit her lip.

And then Lachlin fit his crown at the base of her opening, inching his way forward. Her head fell back against Jax's shoulder at the exquisite pleasure pain. He had barely fit the head of his cock inside her, and she already felt like she was being split in two. She breathed deeply, trying to move past the uncomfortable fullness. Then Jax thrummed his fingers over her swollen clitoris and pleasure flooded her system.

Lachlin was able to slide in another inch. Then he thrust gently back and forth, going no further until her body relaxed around his length. Bit by bit, he pressed forward. Any time she hissed and the pain became too intense, Jax would flick her clit and her tissues would relax, allowing Lachlin deeper and deeper. It felt like it took forever. Lachlin would thrust a little deeper each time, Jax would hiss in her ear, and then stroke her swollen nub. This went on for a good fifteen minutes. By the time Lachlin's full length was inside her, Amaya was in another stratosphere.

Lachlin kissed her deeply once he was fully seated. And then Jax turned her head and took her lips in a torrid mingling that left her breathless. Jax released her lips and Lachlin was there to claim a kiss from him. They growled into each other's mouths. It felt incredible having them both inside her pussy. She could only imagine how good it felt for them; to be this closely connected, with their cocks up against one another, snug inside her pussy. And watching them kiss each other stirred her in ways she hadn't known were possible. It was the hottest thing.

"Ready?" Lachlin asked when he released Jax's mouth.

Jax growled, "Fuck yeah. Her cunt is pouring its juices all over me. Ready, pet?" He nipped her ear.

"Oh god, yes. Please, Sirs, fuck me."

And then they moved; in tandem at first. One would withdraw as the other thrust. It was unbelievable. She never knew this type of pleasure existed. Every nerve ending was lit up like it was the fourth of July. The scent of their combined musk filled the air around them. Amaya wrapped her arms around Lachlin and surrendered herself to the sensation. Thrust, withdraw, thrust, withdraw, over and over again.

Amaya was surrounded in them, filled by them. She never wanted to be anywhere else but within their arms. Then the two men began thrusting together and she nearly lost the edges of her sanity. She was babbling and whimpering. Her nails dug into Lachlin's back as their combined thrusts increased in tempo. Lachlin and Jax were moaning in her ears. With every stroke, her body tightened in on itself. When she came, it was going to be the mother of all orgasms. And as much as she didn't want the ecstasy to end, she felt the edges of her control slipping. She needed to come.

"Oh god, please, Sirs, please let me come," she begged, and then her words turned into a long moan as they pounded harder, faster, making her go crazy.

"Let's let her have it. She's been a good little sub."

"Ahhh," she moaned as waves bombarded her system. She shuddered and clenched at their thrusting cocks as they burrowed deep inside her pussy.

And then they began moving together, fucking her in sync, and every jack-hammered thrust made her see stars. Over and over again they plunged inside; harder, faster, more intense than the last plunge, as though they were attempting to climb inside her, their cocks thundering inside her channel. She loved every minute of it. She dug her nails into Lachlin's back as they used her as the filling in their fuck sandwich.

One minute, she was riding high and the next, an atom bomb hit her system as the mother of all climaxes hit her. She trembled as her pussy clasped and spasmed around their cocks. It was an unending stream of pleasure and her moans were animalistic and guttural as she screamed. Jax and Lachlin groaned as she shook and her pussy continued to clamp and spasm around their shafts. They strained against her as they pounded inside her quivering channel.

"Ahhh, I'm coming, pet. Fuck yeah, milk my cock," Jax roared. Hot streams of liquid flooded her core and his cock jolted.

And then Lachlin jerked, his cock thudded in her dripping pussy, and he moaned.

Neither Dom stopped thrusting until the last drops of their cum filled her pussy. She whined as they withdrew from her. Residual quakes of her climax vibrated through her body.

They repositioned her together until she was nestled between them in bed, pulling the sheets up over them. Amaya fell asleep cradled within their arms, feeling more loved than she had ever felt before.

Chapter Ten

Jax woke first and smiled at Amaya's sweet little body nestled in his arms. Lachlin was at her back, still sleeping like a log. Jax gazed at her precious face and his heart warmed at how right she felt in his arms. She'd had it rough; he understood that, because his own upbringing and abandonment issues were no picnic. But it was her heart, the incredible generosity inside her, that fascinated him the most. After everything she had been through recently, she was still able to love them without reservation. She held nothing of herself back from them, giving herself over into their care with a courage of the heart that was rare. So she'd not had a full time Dom before, and there were gaps in her learning. That was easily fixed… because she was perfect for them. She'd not said any words of love, but he had felt them in her touch.

Jax had loved Lachlin since they were boys in the orphanage together. He had never thought he would want another with the same breathless anticipation. Amaya had wiggled her way in past his defenses. Lachlin had been right. The man usually was, with his steadfast level head, always keeping Jax from jumping without a parachute.

Jax had fought his feelings for Amaya from the get go, but after last night, he was done fighting them. He loved her. She completed his relationship with Lachlin in a way he had never thought possible. She enriched it. A puzzle piece that had been missing had slid into place, and he knew he wanted her with them for the long term.

That meant if she had to join their band, then so be it. He wasn't letting her get away from them. He stroked a hand over her breast, loving the way her nipple beaded at his touch. She moaned, shifted sleepily in his arms, and blinked her eyes open to stare at him.

"Hi," she said, a blush spreading over her cheeks.

"Sleep well, pet?" He pinched and rolled her nipple, loving the way her eyes widened and took on a passionate glaze. Her pink tongue darted out and licked her lips.

"Never better. You?"

"Like a wee babe. I'd like you to go with us to the club. It's for a public scene."

Storm clouds entered her eyes and he spied fear in their depths. "Are you sure you wouldn't rather just stay here?" She stretched like a cat, parting her legs slightly.

"Nice try. I get that you've been avoiding it because of what happened in Amsterdam. But you know the island is perfectly safe. And Lachlin and I will be there right with you every step of the way. It's time. You trust us, don't you?"

"Yes. Absolutely, it's just, I'm—"

He cupped her chin until she had no choice but to look at him. "I know you're scared, pet, but do you honestly think either myself or Lachlin will let anything happen to you? We will protect and keep you from harm."

"Jax, I—" She cut off what she was about to say and instead reached up and brought his head down. Her lips touched his as she showed him with more than words that he mattered to her.

She shifted in his arms until she was plastered to the front of him. He didn't restrain her, instead reveling in the feel of her hands caressing his back. She wrapped a leg around his waist and he hissed at the delicious contact. His cock, the randy bastard that it was, grew until it was so hard he could cut glass with it.

He took over, rolling Amaya onto her back, insinuating himself between her thighs and then, without preamble, penetrated her wet heat. She moaned into his mouth, never breaking contact with his lips. It wasn't fast. He enjoyed the slow fucking. Feeling every flutter of her pussy as it clasped at his dick. Her hands caressed his spine, down to his butt. She grabbed at his ass, her fingers digging into his flesh as she met him thrust for thrust. She undulated her hips beneath him, trying to pull him deeper inside the sweet, succulent heat of her pussy.

And Jax felt like he was in heaven. He never wanted another pussy. Amaya was their sub; now and always. He wasn't letting her go. He poured his feelings into his kiss and the slow and steady fucking he was giving her. As he thrust and withdrew, her little mewls of delight, the way she clutched his ass and tried to pull him deeper, like she wanted him to crawl inside her warm heat, made him feel like the god of sex.

She was the piece to his heart that he hadn't even realized had been missing. He wanted her, and not just now, as he canted his hips and plowed her pussy with a fervent ardor that was starting to override his control, but with him and with Lachlin for all time. He could imagine his child suckling at her breast and it was his turn to groan into her mouth. All of it: the permanence and the future, he wanted it with her.

He released her lips, wanting to watch her passion-filled gaze, the wonder and desire cross her face. All of it made him hungry for more of her. He adjusted his thrusts, increasing his tempo and the force. She gazed at him, her mouth open, her little moans driving him to pummel her pussy harder. Her fingers dug into his ass and he hissed at the pain. He fucked her with a single-minded determination to leave his mark on her heart and soul. He wanted to imprint himself on her heart so that she never wanted another but himself and Lachlin.

He wanted to forge a similar connection like the one she had had from the start with Lachlin, so that she would turn to him in the night as well.

"Jax, oh god," she wailed. Her pussy clenched and quaked around his cock as her climax hit. The pleasure at hearing her call his name made another key fall into place and it ignited a maelstrom inside him. He cradled her in his arms until her body was merely an extension of his and furiously pounded his dick into her quaking heat, pumping his hips in rapid succession. Her moans continued and built into one long stream.

He growled as his cock swelled. He felt every stroke inside her succulent cunt, all the way down his back. His balls tightened as he increased his pace, slamming inside her quivering sheath. It started at the base of his spine; his balls drew up tight, his cock elongated, and his seed spurted in unending waves.

"Ahhh, I'm coming, Amaya," he roared as he strained, feeling his cum pour inside her pussy.

He didn't stop thrusting until his cock began to soften. Her cunt throbbed around his dick and he felt more replete than he had for an age.

When Jax raised himself up on his elbows and looked down at her beautiful face, awash in afterglow, his Dom nature loved her even more. He gave her a tender kiss.

"I must say, that was quite the show. But if you are both done, my poor neglected cock could use some attention," Lachlin said.

Jax and Amaya turned their heads, and a smile was on her lips. Lachlin lay on his side, not hiding his erection. After their lovemaking, Jax needed some recovery time.

"Why don't you take care of Lachlin, pet? We can't have his poor cock falling off from neglect now, can we?"

She shook her head with a grin. "No, we cannot."

"Come ride my neglected cock and make it feel better, love." Lachlin held out his hand.

Jax shifted off her taut body, immediately missing her warmth. Amaya took his hand as Lachlin rolled onto his back and helped her straddle him. Jax groaned as he watched Lachlin fit his wonderful cock, the one Jax had loved for forever, at the entrance to Amaya's cunt, which was still dripping, seeping with his cum.

And then Lachlin thrust, holding Amaya's hips as he embedded his dick in her sheath. Lachlin grimaced at the exquisite pleasure to be found in the bounty of her pussy. It was Jax's turn to watch his two lovers fuck. He loved knowing that his cum was lubricating their fucking. It was so erotic to be a part of their lovemaking, even when he wasn't participating.

Amaya rode Lachlin, rolling and undulating her hips as Lachlin thrust. Lachlin gripped her tits, tweaking the nipples as she ground harder, taking his cock deeper and deeper. She had the stamina to withstand their sexual needs. She was a goddess among subs.

It was beautiful to watch their pleasure in each other. Amaya's head thrown back, her mouth open on a moan as her desire rose. Lachlin's face dark with hunger as he attempted to contain his lust and pumped his hips to give her as much pleasure as possible.

Jax couldn't stand not being a part of it any longer. His cock once again strained for release. Pre-cum leaked from his crown. He grabbed the ever-present tube of lube and then moved into position behind Amaya.

"Lean forward, pet. I find that I need to join you."

Amaya did as he commanded with a groan. Lachlin pulled her to his chest, slowed his thrusts and stilled, buried inside her dripping heat. She was already open for Jax's pleasure, her pretty rosette waiting for his cock. He slathered lube over the puckered hole and then over his erection. Then he pressed the crest against her hole. He hissed as he moved forward into the tight passage. Amaya moaned.

"Breathe, pet, let me in and then we will fuck you until you can't walk."

Amaya whimpered in desire at his words but then did as he bade. She breathed deep, relaxing her body and allowing his cock to slide past the tight ring of muscle. He thrust forward, inch by delicious inch as her body stretched to accommodate his girth. She was so snug and tight he had to grit his teeth or he would shoot his load before they even started to fuck.

Jax could feel Lachlin's cock through her tissues as he furrowed deeper. Lachlin held himself still and Amaya steady until Jax had penetrated her fully. When he nodded at Lachlin, they began to move. Amaya was beyond delirious with passion. She was on the other side, moaning and wailing as they thrust, mumbling incoherently as they pounded.

Jax leaned forward, enjoying the feel of his balls against Lachlin's as they fucked their sub. He pressed forward until they were fucking her with their cocks pistoning in and out of her in hammered thrusts that were sure to send her over the edge soon. He thrust harder, faster, pounding her ass almost brutally.

"Please let me come, Sirs, please. I, oh god," Amaya moaned, and he noticed her fingers digging into Lachlin's chest so hard they would likely leave little marks.

Lachlin gave him a look and said, "What do you say, J, should we let her have it?"

Jax could tell Lachlin was near release, as well. "Well, she has been a good little sub this morning. I think she deserves it, don't you?"

Lachlin nodded. "All right, love, come for us."

He and Lachlin unleashed themselves on her. They rode her like animals intent on one thing and one thing only: pleasure. At her mewled cries of stunned pleasure, Jax rammed his cock inside her grasping ass with a fury that stole his own breath.

"Oh god, oh god, Sirs!" Amaya screamed as she came. Her body vibrated and shook in their arms. Her ass clenched around Jax's cock. Her orgasm set off a chain reaction and he and Lachlin were coming on the next stroke.

"Ahhh, Amaya," he roared as his cum blasted her ass.

Lachlin bellowed, his face contorting into an expression Jax knew well. Lachlin's cum was spilling inside Amaya's pussy and mixing with his.

His cock thudded in her ass, drawing another yelped moan from Amaya.

"Well, that was definitely the best way to wake up. Who wants pancakes?" Lachlin said with a satisfied grin.

"As long as there's bacon," Jax said, "but first, I think a shower is called for, don't you?" He gave Lachlin a look filled with meaning. He was blessed that he didn't always have to communicate his intent verbally.

"I think Jax is right. Our sub definitely needs a shower."

"Yes, Sirs, whatever you want."

Jax kissed her shoulder as he withdrew his dick from her warmth and said in her ear, "Well, I for one plan to clean up all that cum leaking from your pussy… with my tongue."

Amaya whimpered and it made him grin. Then he helped her off Lachlin. Her legs wobbled like a newborn foal and Jax scooped her up into his arms, carting her into the bathroom with Lachlin on his heels. It was quite some time and a few dozen more orgasms later when they finally made breakfast.

Chapter Eleven

Amaya was floating on air for most of the day. Life was as close to idyllic as she'd ever experienced. After their morning in bed and in the shower, she, Jax and Lachlin had plowed through stacks of pancakes and a pound of bacon between the three of them. She justified it with the amount of sex they were having—she needed the carbs and protein if she was to keep up with their fervent demands.

Just thinking about the way Jax had made love to her that morning warmed her heart. Maybe they really did have a future together. The three of them had spent the better part of the day working on a song for the Harbingers' new album. Amaya knew they had asked her to join them in order to make her feel better about her current lack of employment.

And they had both mentioned letting some of the studio execs know she was available to do studio recordings with other bands.

She didn't want to rely on them fully. As much as she was submissive, she had also steered her own course for a long time. She needed to feel wanted, to feel useful, that she was contributing to society. She just wasn't certain it was a good idea for her to become totally dependent on them. No matter how much the men professed to care for her, they'd never spoken about love or commitment beyond their time together on the island. She did believe, given time, that they would both love her. And she wanted the chance for their relationship to deepen that way. But she worried about making herself so dependent that, should they decide to back out, it would crush her. And she knew she was being paranoid and giving in to the fears whispering in the back of her mind but really, could anyone blame her?

Amaya felt complete for the first time in her life with her guys. Not just in the bedroom, which was amazing. Her belly clenched and her sex throbbed with delight at every memory. They made her weak-kneed and she was willing to submit to almost everything they wanted. She did have some reservations about that night, though.

Amaya knew it was her fear of a repeat of what had transpired in Amsterdam, and having to watch her new world crash and burn before it even had the chance to bud and bear fruit. She was putting the final touches on her hair and make-up in the bathroom and her hand trembled. At least she looked hot. She may not feel confident but it didn't show, thankfully.

She had put on the leather bra and panty set under the see-through black fishnet dress. Then she'd applied smoky eye make-up, which she thought made her eyes look larger and more exotic. The finishing touch was a deep burgundy lipstick.

A part of her hoped that her guys would take one look at her in this get up, lose control, and need to fuck her brains out immediately. Then they would never make it out the door to the club—today, at least. She would do anything to forestall that event. She felt the panic rising in her chest even at the thought of going to the club. But that was wishful thinking on her part, and she didn't like playing the ostrich. She had made strides—big ones in her mind—since she had arrived on the island. And much of that was due to Jax and Lachlin.

Her men. Her Doms.

At the knock on the bathroom door, she knew her time was up. "Coming," she said after double-checking her appearance in the mirror one final time.

She walked into the bedroom.

"Christ, Amaya, you look good enough to eat," Jax said, his gaze darkening with desire. There was a definite bulge growing in his leather pants.

"Love, you have outdone yourself getting ready for the club tonight. Makes me almost wish we could keep you to ourselves and stay in," Lachlin murmured, sliding his arm around her waist and pulling her close.

"We could, you know, stay here," she said, leaning into his warmth.

Jax cocked his head to the side. "Amaya, we are going. I understand what you're attempting to do here, pet, and it won't fly." Then he approached her and continued, "We will be by your side the entire night. The scene we have planned is an easy one. This is all about dipping your toes back into the well. It will be cold at first, but we will help you warm it up."

"I'm sorry. I'm just nervous," she admitted and hung her head, feeling pathetic.

Jax kissed her brow. "We know, pet. We should get going before I change my mind and decide to fuck you where you stand." She moaned and Jax chuckled darkly.

They headed out to the cart. Lachlin climbed into the driver's seat and Jax slid into the passenger's side, then patted his lap.

"Come and sit that pretty ass of yours down here, pet."

She did as he bid. Jax placed each of her legs on either side of his so that they were spread in a wide V. As Lachlin stepped on the gas and the cart meandered down the paved path, Jax drew the hem of her skirt up to the top of her leather panties.

"Sir?"

"Relax, pet, I'm just going to finger you and give you a little climax to calm your nerves a bit. So let me in. In fact," he said, "there's nothing you can do about it. Just enjoy."

His hand slid between her legs, toying with the edges of the crotchless panties, and her sex throbbed. Then he dipped his fingers in, stroking through her labia folds. They came away coated with her dew.

"See, you're already drenched. Your pussy is begging for my fingers."

She bit back a moan as his fingers caressed her clit. He toyed with her nub, rubbing his fingers in circles. Her musk scented the air and she writhed on his lap. Need swamped her system. And then he penetrated her pussy, inserting two fingers and thrusting them into her grasping channel. He thrust and she canted her hips.

Then she begged, feeling the hard bulge beneath her ass. "Please fuck me, Sir. Please."

He growled into her ear, leaned her forward slightly and she felt his cock spring forth from his pants. Then he was lifting her and penetrating her. His hands guided her hips and she moaned as she ground her hips in response. She loved his cock. It stretched her tissues almost to the point of pain. She lost sight of where Lachlin was driving them. Her entire world was centered on Jax and the way he was fucking her. This was no sensual love play, but a down and dirty fuck. It was a race to the finish line.

She was coming as Lachlin parked the cart at the hotel. Jax's hot cream filled her channel and she moaned as she came.

When Jax stopped thrusting, Lachlin chimed in, "My turn. No way in hell are you two going to have all the fun."

She cast a baleful eye his way. Lachlin had already undone the laces of his leathers and his cock stood at attention. She moaned as he lifted her off Jax's lap. His semen was leaking from her pussy. And then Lachlin positioned her so that she was straddling him on the seat. He gripped his cock in his hand and guided her down onto his length.

Her eyes nearly rolled back in her head at the exquisite pleasure. His longer cock pushed deeper, almost hitting the lip of her womb. And then he helped her ride him, his fingers digging into her hips as he thrust. Amaya held on, bucking, and rolling her hips, taking his cock in deeper and deeper. She threw her head back as pleasure swelled and crested, her body shattering into a million explosions yet again.

"Oh, god!" Her back arched as he hammered her pussy.

Lachlin latched his mouth around her nipple as he pounded. He bit down on her nipple as he jerked and his shaft thudded in her pussy, sending a myriad of residuals sparks ricocheting through her body as he climaxed.

She collapsed on top of Lachlin, unable to move yet for fear her legs wouldn't support her.

Then Jax kissed her on the forehead. "See? Now you are all calm for the club."

They both helped her up off Lachlin's lap and set her on her feet. Jax followed her out of the

Anya Summers

cart as she adjusted the skirt of her dress back down over her rear.

"Pet, after that display, I think you could walk around the island in the buff," Jax said.

"You would like that, wouldn't you?"

"Absolutely. In fact, after seeing you in that dress that isn't a dress, I might just have to command it," Jax said as he slid his arm around her waist, drawing her to his side.

Lachlin finally joined them, flanking her other side, putting his hand on her rear. As they rode the elevator up to the second floor, Amaya felt like she had been claimed by her Doms. She chose that as a litany, something to repeat in her mind as fear clenched her system.

The three of them made the rounds; Lachlin and Jax speaking with a few Doms. Amaya already knew Deke and Shep. They were on one of the black couches with Yvette on Deke's lap and Shep massaging her feet.

Yvette gave her a wink. Clearly, she was having the time of her life with her two Doms. Not that Amaya blamed her one bit. Now that she had experienced the double trouble of her Doms, she didn't think she could ever go back to just one man.

Jared and Naomi were there, putting on quite the show on the main center stage. Jared had Naomi riding what looked like a bull rider's saddle strapped on top of a big black barrel. She was nude, and there was a dildo in the center of the saddle that

164

she was riding. Jared stood with his feet spread wide. Amaya couldn't see his back but judging by the tension in his shoulders, he was disciplining his little sub. Amaya almost felt sorry for her but knew that Jared was doing it out of love.

Jax pulled her onto one of the nearby couches and Lachlin left them to grab some drinks. He returned with two beers and a white wine for Amaya. He sat on her other side. Both men teased her nipples as they watched the rest of the discipline scene.

Naomi's face was flaming red and there were tears streaming down her face but she appeared resolved to accept the punishment that Jared was doling out. Her body strained and Amaya—as well as everyone else watching the session—could see that she had climaxed on the saddle. She would have tumbled off but Jared was there with a warm blanket to catch her. He carried her over to his throne and sat with her cuddled in his arms. She'd buried her face in his neck.

Amaya wondered whether the little maid was fit for the Master of the island, but then she saw the look on Jared's face as he kissed Naomi. That was the look of a man deeply in love. Her belly tightened. Both of her men had looked at her like that. Did that mean that they were in love with her?

She finished off her glass of wine. "Come on pet, our station is finally ready." Jax helped her to her feet and they led her over to one of the alcoves. This one had a St. Andrew's Cross on it and there was also a fuck bench. Amaya's sex throbbed. What were they going to do? Clearly they planned to restrain her. Would both of them have sex with her here? Everything tended to dissolve around her whenever they made love. Hell, she'd fucked them in a golf cart. That was a new one, even for her.

Her heart rate rose as they entered the alcove. Normally she was so calm, but now that she was here, images of the photos taken of her in Amsterdam flitted across her mind.

"All right, love, strip out of that lovely little thing you call a dress and come over here. We're going to—"

"No. I'm-I'm-I'm so sorry," she stammered as she backed away from the scene area.

"Pet, get back here," Jax ordered.

Panic reached up and grabbed her by the throat. She could hardly breathe. She feared she was going to hyperventilate. She shook her head, tears leaking down her cheeks. She couldn't do it. She didn't want to disappoint them, but her panic overrode her every rational thought process. Before anyone could stop her, she swiveled and ran. She didn't wait for the elevator but took the stairs. The stone steps were cold beneath her bare feet. Amaya raced away with Jax and Lachlin's startled shouts ringing in her ears.

Outside the main hotel, she ran on the path, running as fast as her legs would go. Tears blinded her vision as she ran. She was so grateful for the illuminated path as she went. It guided her footsteps. Her only thought was to escape the panic clawing at her chest. She couldn't go to the club. It was a recipe for disaster. She should have asked them to give her another day or two. Tell them that she wasn't ready to face that when she had already faced so much.

"Get in the cart, Amaya," Jax said in a commanding voice.

She shook her head, her tears falling fast and furious. "No, please, I don't want to go back there. Please don't make me."

Her breath hitched as she kept running.

The white cart swiveled in front of her and she wasn't fast enough to turn. It was Lachlin's arms which corralled her and pulled her into the back seat. She struggled and squirmed on his lap.

"Please don't make me go back there, Sirs, please. I can't do it yet. Please don't make me." She sobbed into Lachlin's chest, hyperventilating as she cried.

"Shush, love, I've got you. We're taking you home. Hush, nothing's going to hurt you, not on our watch."

Lachlin held her close as Jax drove them the rest of the way back to the villa. Amaya knew she had screwed up royally. Was this the point where

167

they would toss her aside because she couldn't be perfect? She tried so hard to be, but somehow it was never enough. She was never good enough.

She was rigid in Lachlin's arms as he carried her into the villa. Jax's stern expression made bats flop around in her belly. Lachlin marched to the couch and sat with her in his lap. His expression mimicked Jax's.

"Let it out, love." Lachlin stroked his hands down her back. "Deep breaths. You are safe and protected. Nothing bad will happen to you."

Lachlin just held her, working the tight kinks from her shoulders, letting the panic that had driven her forward subside and diminish. Jax slid in beside Lachlin, massaging her feet and then her calves. They didn't talk until she had calmed down, and was past the worst part of her attack.

Lachlin tilted her face up to his and said, "We understand why you did what you did, but your delivery of it was unacceptable, love. I want you to understand that if you had been more honest with us and told us as your Doms that you were starting to experience a panic attack, we would have helped you work through it. Even if that meant canceling the scene for the night and just being social at the club for a bit."

"I'm so sorry, I never meant to, I just couldn't think as the panic descended, and everything in me told me to run. I kept seeing those pictures of me in Amsterdam that the conductor waved in my face." She buried her face in his chest.

"I know, which is why we are going to go light on you. But we won't take away the punishment. Even though we know you didn't mean to do it, we cannot help you and do our jobs properly if you don't submit yourself fully."

"But I have," she said.

"Your body, yes, you have in so many ways, and Jax and I adore you for it. But you're holding yourself—the most important part of your surrender and submission—from us. And that starts with trusting us one hundred percent. Have either of us ever given you a reason to believe we would allow harm of any kind to touch you?" Lachlin asked.

"No," she mumbled into his chest, ashamed as a fresh bout of tears started.

Jax murmured, "If you had said to either of us that you were panicking over it, we would have talked about it, but instead you not only ran, but disobeyed our commands in front of the entire club crowd. For that, you will receive thirty swats to that delectable derrière. Fifteen from Lachlin and fifteen from me, understood?"

"Yes, Sirs." She knew she deserved it. They were right, she should have told them she was having a panic attack.

Lachlin shifted her in his arms until her midsection lay over his thighs. Then hands were at

169

the hem of her dress, drawing it up to her waist. Another set of hands drew her panties off completely. A forearm pressed against her lower back, and another held her thighs.

The first spank made her gasp. The second was harder than the first and she braced herself for the third.

"Just let go," Lachlin ordered. He walloped her ass with three more intense strokes. The crack of his palm filled the space, along with her muttered gasps. Somewhere during the latter half of Lachlin's portion of her punishment, Amaya stopped fighting.

They were right. She had been holding herself back out of fear. She'd done what she could to maintain control instead of giving them her full submission. As he tanned her ass ruby red, she melted, letting go of any outcome. She should have trusted them. She couldn't love them if she didn't give them her trust.

And she did trust them. She wasn't as cured of her earlier depression as she had thought. This was all part of it.

Then they transferred her to Jax's lap. His swats were a bit harsher, and she whimpered under each one, but she didn't fight. She didn't have to fight them. She finally had not one but two Doms who were on her side. They'd never once let her down. She was the one who had let them down by

170

not giving them what they needed, which was her full submission.

She offered it to them freely. She couldn't claim to love them if she didn't give them her submission.

When Jax had finished, he said, "Well now, would you look at that? I never thought you would ever surrender and for once, I feel blessed that I was wrong. Come on, pet. I have some delicious torture to add to your punishment for which I'm sure you will be cursing me before long."

Jax turned her in his arms and kissed her. When he broke the kiss, the naked emotion in his gaze rocked her to her core. The seeds of hope sprang to life in her heart. Maybe. Maybe there really was a future with him, with them.

Then Lachlin swooped in for his kiss and it melted her heart. Lachlin moved first, assisting her up off Jax's lap. They led her into the dungeon area.

"Do us a favor, pet, and take the rest of that dress off. The bra too, as much as I admire the way it displays your pretty nipples," Jax said.

She did as he asked without question. As soon as she was done, she stood in a submissive pose with her head down, her hands behind her back, and waited for them. When a hand entered her field of vision, she took it without question. She knew it was Jax, just by the shape of his fingers. They led her to a small metal tower and fastened her arms behind her back in leather cuffs. Then they spread her legs, putting each in an ankle cuff.

A metal arm extended from the tower between her legs and it held a Hitachi vibrating wand, which Jax positioned at her pussy. He went so far as to spread the lips of her labia and place the device squarely up against her clitoris. Amaya shivered. Whatever torture they had in mind, she knew that in the end, it wouldn't hurt her, and would likely end with multiple orgasms for her. Not a bad bargain to appease her two Doms and be what they needed.

"Look at us, pet," Jax commanded.

When she moved her gaze up, both men had disrobed and stood with their proud erections jutting before them. They were downright the most fuckable men. They made her ache to feel them thundering inside her. She panted as their cocks bobbed under her gaze.

"Now, you are to watch me fuck Lachlin. You are not to close your eyes and you are not to come. Do you understand?"

Oh sweet Jesus! "Yes, Sirs. I understand."

"Do not under any circumstances close your eyes, and if you come, Lachlin will fuck me, and only me, and you will be forced to watch but not participate at all tonight."

"Yes, Sirs."

"Good." Then Jax smiled wickedly and turned the vibrating wand on. He put it on a medium

172

setting so it wasn't too fierce but it also wasn't too light. The vibrations stirred her need, making her want to undulate her hips against the vibrating motor.

"Remember, love, eyes on us," Lachlin said as he went into Jax's arms. They kissed one another and Amaya felt a ball of lust slam into her pussy. It was no gentle kiss, either. They held each other close. Their dicks swayed against each other and her pussy throbbed.

Their kiss intensified and they groaned into each other's mouths. Then Jax broke the kiss and ordered Lachlin, "On your knees."

The pleasure on Lachlin's face as he did Jax's bidding was startling. It made Amaya's belly churn in delicious swirls. Jax groaned when Lachlin grabbed his cock, running his hand up and down the shaft a few times before he opened his mouth and took him inside, giving him head.

Jax hissed as he fed his cock into Lachlin's mouth. They seemed to know exactly what the other liked. Jax's hand went to Lachlin's head as he pumped his hips. And Lachlin was in sheer heaven as he sucked Jax's thick shaft. He had no qualms about taking him deep or allowing Jax to be almost brutal in his thrusts.

"Enough," Jax growled. "I want to fuck your ass. Get on the horse."

Lachlin complied, stood, and climbed up on the horse, letting Jax restrain his ankles and wrists.

173

And through it all, the vibrations from the wand were driving Amaya crazy. Her nipples were swollen pebbled points. Her pussy wept as she tried to push past her own rising desire to obey their commands. The wand, combined with watching her two men fuck each other… it wasn't possible that she could last. But she would try.

Jax slathered his cock with lube and then rubbed a bit more on Lachlin's ass. The look on Lachlin's face as Jax pressed his cock into his ass, working his erection inside his back hole until he was easily sliding in and out, was one of the most erotic things Amaya had ever witnessed. Jax's face was fierce with concentration, while Lachlin's was complete, utter bliss. And then Jax began to fuck him in earnest.

The whole scene, watching Jax's cock disappear into Lachlin's ass and the way Jax gripped his hips as he jack-hammered his lover, made her core tighten in on itself. Her clitoris swelled and she moaned, loudly. Both men swiveled their heads and looked at her then.

"Oh god, please Sirs, please let me come." Watching them screw was turning her on in ways she never imagined. And she wanted to participate. She wanted to be underneath them, on top, whichever way they would take her.

Jax chuckled and said, "Not yet, pet."

Lachlin groaned then as Jax turned it up a notch. Her wetness dripped down her thighs. The way she was restrained meant she couldn't move away from the incessant vibrations. She breathed deeply as both men were groaning. Jax's thrusts became more hurried, more violent as his control snapped. They were breathtaking as they fucked. Sinuous and sensual and masculine. Jax was conquering Lachlin with every hammered thrust and it was a thing of beauty.

Lachlin moaned, his semen pouring from his cock as he came. And then Jax trumpeted his release, shouting loudly as he plunged and went rigid.

Amaya whimpered. "Please, Sirs, please let me come."

Jax withdrew from Lachlin's ass, his cock coated with his semen. He undid Lachlin's restraints and then walked to her with utter confidence rolling off him in waves. He shut off the wand's vibrations and moved the metal arm holding the vibrator. Then he knelt before her, his mouth going directly to her pussy like it was a homing beacon. He sucked her engorged, overly sensitive clit into his mouth, his tongue swiping at her juices. He plunged two fingers into her sheath and said around her clit, "Come for me."

Then he bit down on her clit as he thrust his fingers again and again. The pleasure pain combined with the finger fucking and Amaya shattered.

"Oh, god!" she wailed. Her body trembled, her pussy clenching at his fingers, which were still thrusting in her dripping passage.

She'd been strung out for so long that she quickly felt unsatisfied, like she needed something more. Jax helped her off the tower and her legs buckled. Jax followed her down onto the rug until he was between her thighs. One moment, she was empty and the next, Jax plowed past her defenses and thrust his shaft inside. "Oh, Jax!" she cried out as he thrust.

She met him thrust for thrust as they rolled on the carpet. She needed hard, she needed fast, and she needed a lot of him. They ended with her straddled on top of him, riding his shaft like a cowgirl riding her horse. Then Lachlin was there at her back, pressing her forward so that her face was hovering an inch from Jax's.

She hissed at the feel of Lachlin sliding his cock into her back channel. When he moved all the way into her snug ass, Amaya came apart at the seams. The orgasm stole her breath and her ability to think. She became a carnal being that only wanted one thing: for them to keep on fucking her until they were all spent.

"Whatever you do, please don't stop, Sirs."

And the fervor seemed to sweep inside them as they lay on the floor. Jax and Lachlin fucked her like two sailors about to go off to war on the last night of their leave. She hardly knew where one man ended and the other began. All she knew was that she needed them more than she needed air to breathe.

Amaya came three more times before the grand finale. Sweat slicked their bodies; Jax and Lachlin pummeled her holes and grunted, groaned, and fucked with a single-minded determination to wring every drop of pleasure from their bodies.

Amaya could feel her next climax building, her nerve endings frayed and on complete meltdown. Lachlin spurted in her ass, bellowing his completion as he shot his load. It set off a chain reaction in her body. Her ass clenched around his erupting cock, spasming as she came. Her pussy quaked, gripping Jax's cock and trying to milk it of its cum.

"Oh, god," she cried as her body detonated and the world around her dimmed.

She heard Jax shout as he came, thrusting in hammer strokes as he filled her pussy with cum. But she teetered on the edge as her body vibrated and lost the battle as she passed out.

Chapter Twelve

Jax and Lachlin woke first from their tangled heap on the rug. They gently moved Amaya into bed. She mumbled but snuggled deep under the covers. Lachlin had to admit his Dom side was damn proud that they had screwed their sub into oblivion. She had passed out from the pleasure. He felt his chest puff up with pride.

He headed into the bathroom to relieve his bladder, then he planned to climb into bed with their sub and sleep undisturbed for the next twelve hours. He turned from the toilet and found Jax leaning against the bathroom counter with a pensive look on his face.

"Out with it," he said.

"I want to make our arrangement with Amaya more permanent," Jax said.

"How permanent?" Had it worked? Lachlin held his breath.

Jax shot him a bemused expression, raising a sardonic brow. "What can I say, you were right. She is the sub for us. I never thought there would be anyone else in the world for me but you, however, Amaya has proven me wrong."

"I love her," Lachlin admitted. "I hope that won't be an issue. It doesn't mean I love you any less, or that I love her more."

Jax shook his head. "You don't have to explain because I feel the same. I know she has an issue with trust and I think I know how to solve that."

"How?"

"We ask her to marry us," Jax said.

Lachlin's heart shuddered. "You would do that?"

"I love her too. And I think she belongs with us. We understand her like no one else can. I worry about passing her to another Dom who won't understand what she needs." Jax rubbed a hand over his head, mussing up his hair.

"You're sure? Because if we do this and then you get cold feet, it would crush her," Lachlin said. He didn't care which one of them married her legally, as long as she was theirs forever. But he also wanted Jax to understand the gravity of what he was proposing. Jax didn't always look before he leapt, and that could lead to disaster when it came to Amaya. She was still too fragile. Maybe after a few years of their constant love and protection, when she was more certain of them and herself, then he wouldn't have to worry so much.

"I'm sure. In fact, I think there was a part of me that knew I wanted her for the long haul. Since I first fucked her on the beach, neither of us have worn protection, and even if she's on the pill, she still could get pregnant. I want that, I just hadn't realized how much. And I want it with her. We just

179

have to set our plan in motion and make her want to be with us, not only as our sub, but our wife," Jax said.

Hearing Jax say the words, Lachlin walked over to him, wrapping his arms around the man who had been his lover and his best friend practically his whole life. "Thank you."

Jax hugged him back and said, "Best idea you've had in a long time."

He and Jax sat in the bathroom for a while, cultivating their plans and just how they intended to propose before they padded back into the bedroom, each of them slipping into bed with Amaya, one on either side. Lachlin laid his hand over her hip, and Jax put his on top. They were all connected. Lachlin knew deep down that Amaya loved them. It was up to them to convince her that they wanted a lifetime with her.

Lachlin closed his eyes and fell asleep on cloud nine. He had the two people he cared about most in the world with him. And soon they would make it official that she belonged to them in every way—and that they belonged to her right back.

Chapter Thirteen

Amaya awoke the next day and stretched. Her body was blissfully sore, but she adored every ache. She stretched her arms further but didn't encounter either of her men.

That was odd.

She glanced around the bedroom and it was empty. On one of the pillows beside her head was a single red rose and a handwritten note.

Amaya,

We had some errands to run. Stay at the villa and we will be back by midday. Wear the dress we laid out for you on the kitchen table.

L&J

P.S. Don't make me have to spank that beautiful ass of yours. J

She chuckled at his post script note. Jax was just that: Jax. Her heart overflowed with love for them. She was the luckiest woman in the world to have them. Fate was a funny beast. Who would have thought that what had started out as the worst thing in her life would open the doorway for the best? She climbed out of bed, smelling the rose with a bright smile on her lips. Her thigh muscles groaned after yesterday's exertions. She padded naked into the kitchen, where they had laid out one of her little black cocktail dresses with lace detail. What did they have up their sleeves?

It was far more formal than she would have guessed. Were they going to the club? Maybe they were taking her on a date. Not that this island had many options, but her heart swelled with love for them. She had never thought in a million years that she could love two men and want to be with them both. She craved them. Yearned for them when they weren't around.

Happy as a clam, Amaya had breakfast, and then treated herself to an indulgent bubble bath with some Epsom salt to relieve her aching muscles. If her men were taking her on a date and going to be uber romantic, the least she could do was make sure she could thank them properly at the end.

She shaved her legs, and after a long soak, pampered her skin with moisturizer. She painted her toenails and gave herself a facial. She wanted everything to be perfect when Jax and Lachlin returned. She ate a light lunch then finished getting ready, taking time to apply her make-up. She styled her hair so that her normal straight sheet of black hair fell in loose curls over her bare back. She selected her lingerie with care, settling on a pair of black, see-through panties. She opted to go braless because the dress really didn't allow for it and she liked watching their eyes glaze over when they stared at her nipples.

She kept her feet bare, knowing it was more submissive to do so, but in case they allowed her shoes, she had a pair of black stilettos that she carried into the living room. She was looking at the sheet music Lachlin had left on the coffee table when a melody rose up in her breast. She picked up her violin and started to play. Amaya felt the music swell and fill her as she transferred that feeling into her bow. She smiled as she played, caught up in the joy of creation, the joy of playing because she loved it.

They had brought her back to this. For so long, she had forgotten why she had agreed to chase after her career with a dogged determination, forsaking everything else in her life. She loved music. It was a part of her soul. Sometimes the best, and sometimes the worst, for it had made her blind to everything else that was missing in her life.

She played for herself, moving from one song to the next as time dissolved. Music was the air she breathed, the sound of her soul, and she poured her heart into her playing. Mozart and Brahms, then on to Beethoven. It was the reclaiming of a piece of her soul that she thought she had lost: the part of her that had been so eager to audition for the London Symphony Orchestra. She still remembered the day she received the news she'd been given the part. Those had been her dreams, not her father's. She had made it happen.

In the middle of a concerto, her cell phone blared in her purse. With her violin in her hand, she retrieved her phone and answered, putting it on speaker.

183

"Hello," she said.

"Mademoiselle, I need you here for rehearsals," a male voice with a French accent said.

"Francois. It's nice to hear from you, my friend. I'm sorry, but I thought you knew that they fired me," Amaya said, feeling bad. Francois was her favorite conductor.

"I did know, but I don't care. I must have the best violinist in my orchestra and that is you. How soon can you be here?" Francois asked, his voice brooking no room for argument.

"I don't know, things have changed. I'm not sure," she tried to explain.

"I won't take no for an answer. Rehearsals start in one week. I expect you there," Francois all but commanded her over the phone.

She wondered if maybe she should do it, then said, "But the administration, and the pictures."

"You let me deal with the administration. And as for your little betrayer, he's out. I will not have my musicians setting each other up," Francois said with the utter conviction that came with his stature and the fact that the higher ups tended to do anything the man wanted. Bless him. Edward Walsh would get canned, and it made Amaya feel like karma had been served to the rat bastard.

"Francois, you're the best. Truly. I do love you."

"Mon ami, mademoiselle, what would Richard think?" Francois said, referring to his partner of thirty years.

"That I have good taste," she countered, warmth spreading in her chest. All wasn't lost. She had options, she had two Doms she adored, and once she talked to them, discussed her options, they would help her make the right choice for all of them.

Francois barked out a laugh and said, "So do I. One week."

"I'll think about it," she promised him. It was the best she could do until she spoke with Jax and Lachlin.

"No, you'll do it. Don't make me hunt you down," Francois grumbled, with his typical certainty that his command would be followed to the letter.

"Goodbye, Francois." She ended the call.

She spun in a circle, happiness bubbling up in her chest, a scream on the tip of her tongue, only to come face to face with Jax and Lachlin's thunderous expressions.

"So that's it. Just like that, you're going to leave," Lachlin accused her.

"Wait, what? No, I said—"

"We heard enough. Was this just a game to you? Were we just a game?" Lachlin spat, jumping to conclusions before she had even had the chance to process the call.

185

"No, Lachlin, listen, please. He just called and I don't know, maybe it is a good idea that I go back for a little bit, until I can—"

"And what about playing with us? You were on board with going into the studio with us less than twenty-four hours ago. Or do you not remember that?" Lachlin spat. "You know what, fuck this, I'm out."

"Lachlin, wait, please, I don't want you to leave."

He slammed the door as he exited. And she whispered, "I love you. Please don't throw me away."

She crumpled to the ground. The hope she had experienced had been extinguished. Strong arms picked her up and helped her to the couch.

"What did you say?" Jax sat beside her and wiped at her tears with his thumbs.

It was now or never. "I love you, Jax. I love Lachlin, too. I didn't accept the job. I wanted to talk to you both first. And if you didn't want to keep me, then I would have said yes. But I want you both."

"Amaya, I do love you, pet. I didn't expect to. It's Lachlin's fault, actually. He's wanted you since that first time in Scotland. But I was a bit more hard-headed, and couldn't see that you belong with us. Give him some time, love. He will come around."

"You love me?" she asked.

"Yeah, I do. So does he, otherwise he wouldn't have stormed out the way he did."

"But I need to go to him and tell him. I can't let him think—"

"Not tonight. Give him tonight. We have plans, you see, for the three of us. But that's for another night as well."

At Jax's cryptic words, she nodded. What a blunder she had made of everything. "Tell me how I can make it right, how I get him to come back to us."

"Well, now that's what I want to hear. But first, are you sure you don't want to go back to the orchestra? Lachlin and I can make adjustments if that's the case. If it's what you truly want, then we will support you in that."

She smiled. "When did you become the levelheaded one?"

He chuckled.

Did she want to take the job with the orchestra? Two weeks ago, she would have jumped at the chance. But now, she wasn't so certain. The fact was that Jax was willing to see her side of things and give her the choice, when for her, it wasn't a tough decision. Her life with the orchestra had ended, at least on a full-time basis. Maybe she could be a guest violinist on some occasions. But she wanted to make her own music, and she wanted to make more of it with Jax and Lachlin.

She looked him in the eyes and said, "No, I want to go into the studio with you two. I might be a guest violinist with the orchestra, maybe for a week or a performance, but that's not what I want full-time anymore. And I don't think it was what I wanted for a long time, because otherwise I wouldn't have been so careless and reckless in Amsterdam so as to have been caught the way I was. I think I wanted it to implode on some level because I wasn't happy anymore."

"You're sure?"

"Yeah, I am. Jax, I don't want to give him tonight. I'll go stir crazy over it and panic."

"Let's go find him. And by the way, you look sexy as hell in that dress." He gave her a quick kiss as he set her on her feet.

"You should see what I have on underneath," she teased.

"I plan to, pet, and will make you regret teasing me. Just having your ass snug up against my cock is enough to make me hard. I should bend you over the couch and fuck you before we go hunting for Lachlin."

"I promise you can do just that as soon as we find him."

They took the golf cart as they searched the island. Every passing moment they drove and didn't find him, Amaya's anxiety rose, to the point where Jax said, "Relax, would you? You're making me nervous."

"Where would you go if you were him?"

"Probably to the pub."

"Well, there's no pub but there is a bar in the club," she said.

"Let's look there." Jax drove the golf cart as fast as the motor would allow. He parked it right next to the elevator, not caring that it wasn't a designated spot.

They rode up the elevator, Amaya's stomach tied in knots. It was barely seven and the club had a smattering of patrons but it would begin to fill shortly. Immediately her gaze zeroed in on one patron. At the bar, lifting a beer to his lips, was Lachlin. Jax held her steady as they approached. She was thankful for his strength because she felt like she was going to pass out.

Lachlin spied her and his face turned to stone. "Just leave. I don't want to talk to you. And you should probably just pack your belongings and stay at the hotel until you head back to London. Easier this way."

With her heart in her throat, she stopped two feet away and she said, "Actually, I was thinking Australia would be a better fit. And I don't want to stay in the hotel."

Lachlin shook his head and snarled, "Cut the shit, Amaya. I realize you are living out some fantasy but it's my life. Why won't you just leave me in peace?"

Thank goodness Jax was hovering at her back, feeding her the strength she needed. She practically shouted, her own fury riding her system, "Because I love you, you bloody moron!"

Lachlin stilled in his chair, his beer halfway to his mouth. He placed the bottle back on the bar, swiveled his body and climbed off the stool, approaching her. With Jax behind her, she couldn't back away and had to face him as he demanded, "What did you say?"

"I love you, you idiot. I don't want to go to London or play in the orchestra. I want you and Jax. I want to be with you." She looked at him with her heart in her throat. If he turned her away now, she didn't know how she would go on.

Then his hands cupped her face. His eyes were bluer than she'd ever seen and he asked, "Are you sure, love?"

Her confidence built under his touch and she didn't bat an eye. "Absolutely. And I can prove it."

"How?" Lachlin asked, his voice going low.

"Do a scene with me, here, now. You and Jax with me." It wasn't just about her needs, but theirs, too. They needed her to submit to them, to allow them to master her with a scene at the club. And to show Lachlin that he meant the world to her, her panic attacks could take a hike.

His smile was breathtaking as he said, "I thought you'd never ask."

190

Her Music Masters

Chapter Fourteen

Jax and Lachlin led her over to the nearest alcove that had a suspension bar in the center. Jax gave her a look of such love for getting Lachlin to join them, she blushed under his heated gaze. But it was Lachlin who would control the scene. She assumed the position, with her arms behind her back.

"Very pretty. Out of the clothes, love. As gorgeous as you look in this little black number, you look better wearing nothing at all," Lachlin commanded.

Her hands went to the zipper on her dress, and her fingers fumbled with it. Jax murmured, coming up behind her, "Here, let me, pet. I'm dying to see what you have on underneath… Oh, fuck. It's a good damn thing I didn't know, because then I would have fucked you over the couch."

Jax helped her strip as Lachlin prepared the suspension bar. Then he was putting her hands in leather cuffs with their initials worked into the leather—his and Jax's cuffs that Jax had withdrawn from his back pocket, bless him, showing everyone in the club she belonged to them—and then he attached them to the bar above her head. It raised her body up almost uncomfortably and she had to stand on her toes. Jax and Lachlin fit a block under each foot, relieving the pressure on her shoulders. They didn't bind her feet.

Lachlin strode around her, still in his suit pants. His chest was bare and he had removed his belt, so his pants rode low on his hips, exposing his victory lines.

"Give yourself over to us, love. We are just going to use the flogger on you. We'll experiment with other toys later." He caressed her face. "Focus on us, just us, understood?"

"Yes, Sir."

Lachlin took one of the floggers from Jax, who gave her a wink and walked out of her line of sight. Then Lachlin stood before her. The strands of the flogger swayed as he approached and her belly tightened.

"Remember your safeword," he said, gazing at her with love in his eyes.

She nodded and said, "Yes, Sirs."

Then Lachlin ran the leather falls over the front of her body, teasing her with the flogger. Jax did the same on her back, starting at her shoulders and working his way down. They caressed her with the leather strands, lulling her body into a hazy space. She was unprepared for the first crack of the leather as the stroke landed on her rear. Then another thudded against her left breast. They worked together with their floggers, driving her body up a cliff. She didn't see the crowd that began to form but kept her focus on Lachlin.

193

Over and over, they cracked the leather strands against her skin. It felt like her body had lava thundering through her veins. The burning sensation of each strike transmuted and sent a direct line of consummate pleasure straight to her pussy. Her moans increased as they thwacked her and her mind floated above the scene. She moaned and writhed at their touch, her body nearing an intense, shimmering precipice. It was beautiful in its light and in its form.

Her moans crescendoed as her body tightened in on itself and she spiraled and sagged at the release. Then the flogging stopped and she realized tears were streaming down her face. She floated with a sense of peace. She was where she belonged and with the men she belonged to. Lachlin's face moved in front of hers and the look her gave her made her knees tremble.

"I love you, Amaya. Forgive me for jumping to conclusions."

Her tears fell in earnest. He did love her.

"Say something, love."

"Take me home and make love to me," she whispered. She didn't want their lovemaking on display, but for them and them alone.

"I thought you'd never ask," Lachlin said.

Jax and Lachlin undid her cuffs from the suspension bar. Jax wrapped a warm blanket around her, but it was Lachlin who scooped her up in his arms and carried her past their clapping audience. She rested her head on his firm chest, happier than she had ever been.

Lachlin held her as Jax drove them home.

Once they were safely ensconced in the villa, Lachlin and Jax surprised her when they deposited her on the couch. She hissed when she put her weight on her tender rear. She glanced between the two men. Both wore an expression she'd never seen before, and fear licked at the edges of her composure.

"Okay, Sirs, what's going on?"

Jax and Lachlin nodded at each other then, in unison, got down on one knee. Each of them picked up one of her hands. It was Jax who spoke first. "Amaya, I love you, pet, and I want you beside me, loving me in that way you do, forever."

Then Lachlin said, "Amaya, I think I loved you from the very beginning, with your sweet surrender in Scotland all those months ago. Finding you again, and getting the chance to truly love you, feeling how much you love me in return is something I don't ever want to do without or lose again."

"I do love you both so much. I owe you both so much. You brought me back to life," she whispered.

"Hush, love, let me finish," Lachlin commanded before continuing. "I—we—want forever with you if you'll have us. Marry us, Amaya. Be our wife, and our submissive, forever."

She glanced between Jax and Lachlin and what she saw made her breath hitch. They really did love her. "Yes," she blurted, as happy tears leaked over her cheeks.

"Yeah, you're sure?" Lachlin asked.

"Dude, she said yes, shut up. Don't make her change her mind!" Jax chastised him.

"Like you're going to get rid of me that easily," she said and then did something that made both her men moan. She dropped the blanket.

When they both leaned in for a kiss, she said, "Would my Sirs please love me in our bed now?"

"I think we can arrange that," Jax murmured and was the first to stand, pulling her to her feet. But he was too slow for Lachlin, who hoisted her into her arms. She hissed at the contact.

"We'll adjust so none of the welts hurt, love," Lachlin said, and carried her over to their bed. Jax was already there, stripping the covers down and climbing in.

Lachlin lay her on her side, facing him, and followed her in. Jax slid up behind her. Lachlin claimed her lips in a sweet mingling that quickly escalated into a hot, passionate kiss which made her purr into his mouth. When he broke the kiss, he said, "You're ours now and forever."

"My turn," Jax growled, tilting her head back, and he devoured her mouth, plundering the very depths of her soul with his kiss.

Lachlin stroked the sensitive flesh between her thighs. "You're still drenched from the scene, love, so you won't mind if we skip the foreplay?"

She gave him a look filled with all her love and said, "I want you to fuck me, Sirs."

They groaned, and Lachlin covered her lips with his as Jax slathered lube over her rosette. Lachlin teased her clit. Jax growled as he fit his cock against her puckered rear and thrust, working his cock into her back channel. Lachlin continued to stroke her clit, rubbing and driving her crazy until Jax had his turgid shaft embedded in her ass to the hilt.

"My turn," Lachlin growled, fitting his length at her pussy entrance and thrusting. Her sheath drew him deeper inside as he pushed.

"I'd like to apologize for what will most likely be an abbreviated performance, pet," Jax said.

Once Lachlin's length was buried in her pussy, she moaned. They felt so good. And then they began to thrust inside her, driving her mindless. Over and over they thrust, harder, faster, their tempos increasing. They loved her, their arms clasping each other's. The three of them had an unbreakable bond. Amaya mewled at the glorious feel of her men pounding inside her channels, intent on bring her the most exquisite ecstasy. Their movements became sinuous as they tried to draw out their lovemaking, and each Dom took turns

197

claiming her mouth as their own. She poured her love into her kisses, loving them, holding them close.

"Come for us, love," Lachlin ordered on a groan.

They took her body, plunging their cocks in syncopated rhythm, in a musical number as old as time. Amaya's body crested the beautiful peak and shattered as she climaxed. Jax and Lachlin followed her, filling her with their cream and moving until she knew, without any doubt, that they were her music Masters.

Epilogue
Christmas Morning

Amaya checked her dress in the mirror one more time. She couldn't wait to see the expression on Jax and Lachlin's faces. It never ceased to thrill her how much they loved seeing her in lingerie. And this morning, she had dressed as a very naughty Mrs. Claus. She stared at the little box that was four inches long and wrapped. She had an important gift for her future husbands to open.

She knew she couldn't delay anymore without Jax storming into the bathroom. That one was always impatient to see her latest outfit so he could, in his words, 'fuck her until her legs fell off'—not that she minded being on the receiving side of his voracious sexual appetite.

She headed into their bedroom. Jax and Lachlin had quickly moved her into their home in Australia, letting her decorate it to her heart's content.

Jax gave a low whistle. "Pet, I plan to strip you out of that get up with my teeth."

Her belly fluttered as she approached, holding the long white box with the red bow.

Lachlin helped her up into bed, and said, "You're stunning, love, and I for one can't wait to get you out of this delightful costume."

"Yes, Sirs, you can do all that, but first, Merry Christmas." She held the box out to them, her stomach rolling.

"This is for both of us?" Jax said.

"Uh-huh."

"Amaya, you didn't have to get us anything," Lachlin said.

"I know, would you just open the damn thing?" she said, exasperated.

"Demanding little sub. If it weren't Christmas, I'd have to spank you for that." Jax gave her a heated look.

Lachlin removed the lid and both her men stared agape at what was in the box. Lachlin shot her a glance, hope swimming in his eyes. "Is that what I think it is?"

She nodded her head, tears pricking the corners of her eyes.

"We're having a baby, pet?" Jax asked.

"Yeah. How do you both feel about that?" she asked.

"But I thought you were on the pill," Lachlin said, his disbelief evident. And then she noticed his hands were shaking. Who would have thought her steadfast and stalwart Dom would be reduced to putty?

"Remember when we first met, I was a little out of sorts? Well, my first week at Pleasure Island, before you guys arrived, I didn't take my pill.

Apparently that was enough to make it ineffective when we first got together."

Jax and Lachlin glanced at each other and then whooped, pulling her into their arms. She found herself flat on her back in bed, staring up at their beaming faces.

"This is the most precious gift, love." Lachlin kissed her tenderly, laying his hand over her still flat abdomen.

Then it was Jax's turn. He gave her a rakish grin and his eyes were filled with wonder, his hand joining Lachlin's on her belly as he said, "Ditto on what Lachlin said. I love you, pet. I think this means we need to speed up that wedding so our child is protected."

"Whatever my Sirs want," she said, feeling her heart, which she once thought she had lost completely, overflow with love for her men.

And then Jax kissed her and she lost the ability to think or do anything but surrender to their incredible love.

The End

Anya Summers

Born in St. Louis, Missouri, Anya grew up listening to Cardinals baseball and reading anything she could get her hands on. She remembers her mother saying if only she would read the right type of books instead binging her way through the romance aisles at the bookstore, she'd have been a doctor. While Anya never did get that doctorate, she graduated cum laude from the University of Missouri-St. Louis with an M.A. in History.

Anya is a bestselling and award-winning author published in multiple fiction genres. She also writes urban fantasy and paranormal romance under the name Maggie Mae Gallagher. A total geek at her core, when she is not writing, she adores attending the latest comic con or spending time with her family. She currently lives in the Midwest with her two furry felines.

Visit her website here:
www.anyasummers.com

Visit her on social media here:
Http//www.facebook.com/AnyaSummersAuthor
Twitter: @AnyaBSummers

Don't miss these exciting titles by
Anya Summers and Blushing Books!

Dungeon Fantasy Club Series

Her Highland Master, Book 1
To Master and Defend, Book 2
Two Doms for Kara, Book 3
His Driven Domme, Book 4
Her Country Master, Book 5
Love Me, Master Me, Book 6
Submit To Me, Book 7
Her Wired Dom, Book 8

Pleasure Island Series

Her Master and Commander, Book 1
Her Music Masters, Book 2

Made in the USA
Lexington, KY
17 August 2017